NOVEMBER JOE

NOVEMBER JOE

DETECTIVE
OF THE WOODS

H. HESKETH-PRICHARD

COACHWHIP PUBLICATIONS
Landisville, Pennsylvania

November Joe, by H. Hesketh-Prichard.
Copyright © 2010 Coachwhip Publications
First published 1913

ISBN 1-61646-013-X
ISBN-13 978-1-61646-013-6

Cover Image: Cabin on Lake Louise © Harris Shiffman
Cover Image: Hunting Rifle © Valerij Kalyuzhnyy

COACHWHIPBOOKS.COM

CONTENTS

1 · Sir Andrew's Advice   7

2 · November Joe   13

3 · The Crime at Big Tree Portage   19

4 · The Seven Lumber-Jacks   34

5 · The Black Fox Skin   51

6 · The Murder at the Duck Club   73

7 · The Case of Miss Virginia Planx   91

8 · The Hundred Thousand Dollar Robbery   108

9 · The Looted Island   125

10 · The Mystery of Fletcher Buckman   139

11 · Linda Petersham   157

12 · Kalmacks   164

13 · The Men of the Mountains   169

14 · The Man in the Black Hat   177

15 · The Capture   182

16 · The City or the Woods?   187

1

SIR ANDREW'S ADVICE

It happened that in the early autumn of 1908 I, James Quaritch, of Quebec, went down to Montreal. I was at the time much engaged in an important business transaction, which, after long and complicated negotiations, appeared to be nearing a successful issue. A few days after my arrival I dined with Sir Andrew McLerrick, the celebrated nerve specialist and lecturer at McGill University, who had been for many years my friend.

On similar occasions I had usually remained for half an hour after the other guests had departed, so that when he turned from saying the last good-bye, Sir Andrew found me choosing a fresh cigar.

"I cannot call to mind, James, that I invited you to help yourself to another smoke," he said.

I laughed.

"Don't mention it, Andrew; I am accustomed to your manners. All the same—"

He watched me light up. "Make the most of it, for it will be some time before you enjoy another."

"I have felt your searching eye upon me more than once to-night. What is it?"

"My dear James, the new mining amalgamation the papers are so full of, and of which I understand that you are the leading spirit, will no doubt be a great success, yet is it really worth the sacrifice of your excellent health?"

"But I feel quite as usual."

"Quite?"

"Well, much as usual."

Upon this Sir Andrew bent his pronounced eyebrows and brilliant dark eyes upon me and put me through a catechism.

"Sleep much as usual?"

"Perhaps not," I admitted unwillingly.

"Appetite as good as usual?"

"Oh, I don't know."

"Tush, man, James! Stand up!" Thereupon he began an examination which merged into a lecture, and the lecture in due course ended in my decision to take a vacation immediately,—a long vacation to be spent beyond reach of letter or telegram in the woods.

"That's right! that's right!" commented Sir Andrew. "Nothing will do you more good than to forget all these mining reports and assays in an elemental moose-hunt. What do the horns of that fellow with the big bell, which you have hanging in your office, measure?"

"Fifty-nine inches."

"Then go and shoot one with a spread of sixty."

"I believe you are right," said I,—for in the short periods I have been able to spare from my business, I have made many hunting trips, and know that there is nothing like them for change of thought— "but the worst of it is that my guide, Noel Tribonet, is laid up with rheumatism and will certainly not be fit to go with me just now. Indeed, I doubt if he will ever be much good in the woods again."

"But what if I can recommend you a new man?"

"Thanks, but I have had the trouble of training Noel already."

Once again Sir Andrew allowed his penetrating black eyes to rest upon me. Then he broke into his short, rare laugh.

"I can guarantee that you will not find it necessary to train November Joe."

"November Joe?"

"Yes, do you know him?"

"Curiously enough, I do. He was with me as dish-washer when I was up with Tom Todd some years ago in Maine. He was a boy then."

"What did you think of him?"

"I hadn't much opportunity of judging. Todd kept him in camp cooking most of the time. But I do remember that once when we were on the march and were overtaken by a very bad snowstorm, Todd and the boy had a difference of opinion as to the direction we should take."

"And Joe was right?"

"He was," said I. "Todd didn't like it at all."

"Tom Todd had quite a reputation, hadn't he? Naturally he would not like being put right by a boy. Well, that must be ten years ago, and Joe's twenty-four now."

"And a good man in the woods, you say?"

"None better. The most capable on this continent, I verily believe."

I was surprised at Sir Andrew's superlatives, for he was the last man to overstate his case.

"What makes you say that?"

"A habit of speaking the truth, my dear friend. If Joe is free and can go with you, you will get your moose with the sixty-inch horns, I have very little doubt."

"I am afraid there is very slight chance of his being free. You must not forget it's just the beginning of the still-hunting season."

"I know that, but I believe he was retained by the Britwells, who employed him last year, and now at the last minute old man Britwell has decided that he is too busy to go into camp this fall. But there may still be this difficulty. I understand that November Joe has entered into some sort of contract with the Provincial Police."

"With the police?" I repeated.

"Yes. He is to help them in such cases as may lie within the scope of his special experience. He is, indeed, the very last person I should like to have upon my trail had I committed a murder."

I laughed.

"You think he'd run you down?"

"If I left a sign or a track behind me, he would. He is a most skilled and minute observer, and you must not forget that the

speciality of a Sherlock Holmes is the everyday routine of a woodsman. Observation and deduction are part and parcel of his daily
existence. He literally reads as he runs. The floor of the forest is
his page. And when a crime is committed in the woods, these facts
are very fortunate."

"In what way?"

"My dear James, have you never given any consideration to the
markedly different circumstances which surround the wide subject of crime and its detection, where the locality is shifted from a
populous or even settled country to the loneliness of some wild
region? In the midst of a city, any crime of magnitude is very fre-
quently discovered within a few hours of its committal."

"You mean that the detectives can get after the guilty person
while his trail is fresh?"

"Yes, but in the woods it is far otherwise. There Nature is the
criminal's best ally. She seems to league herself with him in many
ways. Often she delays the discovery of his ill-doing; she covers
his deeds with her leaves and her snow; his track she washes away
with her rain, and more than all she provides him with a vast area
of refuge, over which she sends the appointed hours of darkness,
during which he can travel fast and far. Life in the wilderness is
beautiful and sweet, if you will, but it has its sombre places, and
they are often difficult indeed to unveil."

"All things considered, it is surprising that so many woods
crimes are brought home to their perpetrators."

"There you are forgetting one very important point. As you
know, my profession, that of medicine, touches, at one point, very
closely upon the boundaries of criminal law, and this subject of
woods crimes has always possessed a singular fascination for me.
I have been present at many trials and the most dangerous witnesses that I have ever seen have been men of the November Joe
type, that is, practically illiterate woodsmen. Their evidence has a
quality of terrible simplicity; they give minute but unanswerable
details; they hold up the candle to truth with a vengeance, and this,
I think, is partly due to the fact that their minds are unclouded
by any atmosphere of make-believe; they have never read any

sensational novels; all their experiences are at first-hand; they bring forward naked facts with sledge-hammer results."

I had listened to Sir Andrew with interest, for I knew that his precise and accurate mind was not easily influenced to the expression of a definite opinion.

"For some years," he continued, "I have studied this subject, and there is nothing that I would personally like to do better than to have the opportunity of watching November Joe at work. Where a town-bred man would see nothing but a series of blurred footsteps in the morning dew, an ordinary dweller in the woods could learn something from them, but November Joe can often reconstruct the man who made them, sometimes in a manner and with an exactitude that has struck me as little short of marvellous."

"I see he has interested you," said I, half smiling.

"I confess he has. Looked at from a scientific standpoint, I consider him the perfect product of his environment. I repeat there are few things I would enjoy more than to watch November using his experience and his supernormal senses in the unravelling of some crime of the woods."

I threw the stump of my cigar into the fire.

"You have persuaded me," I said; "I will try to make a start by the end of the week. Where is Joe to be found?"

"As to that, I believe you might get into touch with him at Harding's Farm, Silent Water, Beauce.

"I'll write to him."

"Not much use. He only calls for letters when he feels inclined."

"Then I'll cable."

"He lives twenty-seven miles from the nearest office."

"Still they might send it on to him."

"Perhaps; but it is a lonely part of the country, and messengers are likely to be scarce."

"Then I'll go to Harding's and arrange the trip by word of mouth."

"That would certainly be the best plan, and, anyhow, the sooner you get into the woods, the better. Besides, you will be more likely to secure Joe by doing that, as he is inclined to be shy of strangers."

I rose and shook hands with my host.

"Remember me to Joe," said he. "I like that young man. Good-bye and good luck."

2
November Joe

Along the borders of Beauce and Maine, between the United States and Canada, lies a land of spruce forest and of hardwood ridges. Here little farms stand on the edge of the big timber, and far beyond them, in the depths of the woodlands, lie lumber-camps and the wide-flung paths of trappers and pelt-hunters.

I left the cars at Silent Water and rode off at once to Harding's, the house of the Beauce fanner where I meant to put up for the night. Mrs. Harding received me genially and placed an excellent supper before me. While I was eating it a squall blew up with the fall of darkness, and I was glad enough to find myself in safe shelter.

Outside the wind was swishing among the pines which enclosed the farmhouse, when, inside, the bell of the telephone, which connected us with St. George, forty miles distant, rang suddenly and incongruously, high above the clamour of the forest noises.

Mrs. Harding took up the receiver, and this is what I heard.

"My husband won't be home to-night; he's gone into St. George. . . . No, I've no one to send. . . . But how can I? There is no one here but me and the children. . . . Well, there's Mr. Quaritch, a sport, staying the night. No, I couldn't ask him."

I came forward.

"Why not?" I inquired.

Mrs. Harding shook her head as she stood still holding the receiver. She was a matron of distinct comeliness, and she cooked amazingly well.

"You can ask me anything," I urged.

"They want some one to carry a message to November Joe," she explained. "It's the Provincial Police on the 'phone."

"I'll go."

"Joe made me promise not to send any sports after him," she said doubtfully. "They all want him now he's famous."

"But November Joe is rather a friend of mine. I hunted with him years ago when he lived on the Montmorency."

"Is that so?" Her face relaxed a little. "Well, perhaps . . ." she conceded.

"Of course, I'll carry the message."

"It's quite a way to his place. November doesn't care about strangers; he's a solitary man. You must follow the tote-road you were on to-day fifteen miles, turn west at the deserted lumber-camp, cross Charley's Brook, Joe lives about two acres up the far bank." She lifted the receiver. "Shall I say you'll go?"

"By all means."

A few seconds later I was at the 'phone taking my instructions. It appeared that the speaker was the Chief of Police in Quebec, who was, of course, well known to me. I will let you have his own words.

"Very good of you, I'm sure, Mr. Quaritch. Yes, we want November Joe to be told that a man named Henry Lyon has been shot in his camp down at Big Tree Portage, on Depot River. The news came in just now, telephoned through by a lumber-jack who found the body. Tell Joe, please, success means fifty dollars to him. Yes, that's all. Much obliged. Yes, the sooner he hears about it, the better. Goodnight."

I hung up the receiver, turned to Mrs. Harding, and told her the facts. That capable woman nodded decisively.

"You won't have much time to lose, then. I'll put you up a bite to eat."

As I hastily got my things together, I began asking questions about Joe.

"So November is connected with police work now?"

Mrs. Harding answered me with another question.

"Didn't you read in the newspapers about the 'Long Island Murder'?"

I remembered the case at once; it had been a nine days' wonder of headline and comment, and now I wondered how it was that I had missed the mention of Joe's name.

"November was the man who put together that puzzle for them down in New York," Mrs. Harding went on. "Ever since they have been wanting him to work for them. They offered him a hundred dollars a month to go to New York and take on detective jobs there."

"Ah, and what had he to say to that?"

"Said he wouldn't leave the woods for a thousand."

"Well?"

"They offered him the thousand."

"With what result?"

"He started out in the night for his shack. Came in here as he passed, and told my husband he would rather be tied to a tree in the woods for the rest of his life than live on Fifth Avenue. The lumber-jacks and the guides hereabouts think a lot of him. Now you'd best saddle Laura—that's the big grey mare you'll find in the near stall of the stable—and go right off. There'll be a moon when the storm blows itself out."

By the help of the lantern I saddled Laura and stumbled away into the dark and the wind. For the chief part of the way I had to lead the mare, and the dawn was grey in the open places before I reached the deserted lumber-camp, and all the time my mind was busy with memories of November. Boy though he had been when I knew him, his personality had impressed itself upon me by reason of a certain adequate quietness with which he fulfilled the duties, many and disagreeable, which bearded old Tom Todd took a delight in laying upon his young shoulders.

I remembered, too, the expression of humour and mocking tolerance which used to invade the boy's face whenever old Tom was overtaken by one of his habitual fits of talking big. Once when Tom spoke by the camp-fire of some lake to which he desired to guide me, and of which he stated that the shores had never been trodden by white man's foot, Joe had to cover his mouth with his hand.

When we were alone, Todd having departed to make some necessary repairs to the canoe, I asked Joe what he meant by laughing
at his elders.

"I suppose a boy's foot ain't a man's anyways," remarked Joe
innocently, and more he would not say.

In fact, it was with such memories as these that I amused myself as I tramped forward over the rough paths. And now Joe was
grown up into a man who had been heard of, not only within the
little ring of miles that composed his home district, but a little also
out in the great world beyond.

The sun was showing over the tree-tops when I drew rein by
the door of the shack, and at the same moment came in view of the
slim but powerful figure of a young man who was busy rolling some
gear into a pack. He raised himself and, just as I was about to speak,
drawled out,—

"My! Mr. Quaritch, you! Who'd a' thought it?"

The young woodsman came forward with a lazy stride and gave
me welcome with a curious gentleness that was one of his charac-
teristics, but which left me in no doubt as to its geniality.

I feel that I shall never be able to describe November. Suffice it
to say that the loose-knit boy I remembered had developed into
one of the finest specimens of manhood that ever grew up among
the balsam trees; near six feet tall, lithe and powerful, with a neck
like a column, and a straight-featured face, the sheer good looks
of this son of the woods were disturbing. He was clearly also not
only the product but the master of his environment.

"Well, well, Mr. Quaritch, many's the time I've been thinking
of the days we had with old Tom way up on the Roustik."

"They were good days, Joe, weren't they?"

"Sure, sure, they were!"

"I hope we shall have some more together."

"If it's hunting you want, I'm glad you're here, Mr. Quaritch.
There's a fine buck using around by Widdeney Pond. Maybe we
will get a look at him come sunset, for he 'most always moves out of
the thick bush about dark." Then humour lit a spark in his splendid
grey eyes as he looked up at me. "But we'll have a cup o' tea first."

November Joe's (by the way, I ought to mention that his birth in the month of November had given him his name), as I say, November Joe's weakness for tea had in the old days been a target upon which I had often exercised my faculty for irony and banter. The weakness was evidently still alive. I smiled; perhaps it was a relief to find a weak point in this alarmingly adequate young man.

"I had hoped to have a hunt with you, November," said I. "Indeed, that is what I came for, and there's nothing I'd like better than to try for your red-deer buck to-night, but while I was at Harding's there was a ring-up on the 'phone, and the Provincial Police sent through a message for you. It appears that a man named Henry Lyon has been shot in his camp at Big Tree Portage. A lumberman found him, and 'phoned the news into Quebec. The Chief of Police wants you to take on the case. He told me to say that success would mean fifty dollars."

"That's too bad," said Joe. "I'd sooner hunt a deer than a man any day. Makes a fellow feel less bad-like when he comes up with him. Well, Mr. Quaritch, I must be getting off, but you'll be wanting another guide. There's Charley Paul down to St. Amiel."

"Look here, November, I don't want Charley Paul or any other guide but you. The fact of the matter is, that Sir Andrew McLerrick, the great doctor who was out with you last fall, has told me that I have been overdoing it and must come into the woods for rest. I've three months to put in, and from all I hear of you, you won't take three months finding out who murdered Lyon."

Joe looked grave. "I may take more than that," said he, "for maybe I'll never find out at all. But I'm right pleased, Mr. Quaritch, to hear you can stay so long. There's plenty of grub in my shack, and I dare say that I shan't be many days gone."

"How far is it to Big Tree Portage?"

"Five miles to the river and eight up it."

"I'd like to go with you."

He gave me one of his quick smiles. "Then I guess you'll have to wait for your breakfast till we are in the canoe. Turn the mare loose. She'll make Harding's by afternoon."

Joe entered the shack and came out again with one or two articles. In five minutes he had put together a tent, my sleeping-things, food, ammunition, and all necessaries. The whole bundle he secured with his packing-strap, lifted it and set out through the woods.

3
The Crime at Big Tree Portage

I have sometimes wondered whether he was not irked at the prospect of my proffered companionship, and whether he did not at first intend to shake me off by obvious and primitive methods.

He has in later days assured me that neither of my suppositions was correct, but there has been a far-off look in his eyes while he denied them, which leaves me still half-doubtful.

However these things may be, it is certain that I had my work, and more than my work, cut out for me in keeping up with November who, although he was carrying a pack while I was unloaded, travelled through the woods at an astonishing pace.

He moved from the thighs, bending a little forward. However thick the underbrush and the trees, he never once halted or even wavered, but passed onward with neither check nor pause. Meanwhile, I blundered in his tracks until at last, when we came out on the bank of a strong and swiftly flowing river, I was fairly done, and felt that, had the journey continued much longer, I must have been forced to give in.

November threw down his pack and signed to me to remain beside it, while he walked off downstream, only to reappear with a canoe.

We were soon aboard her. Of the remainder of our journey I am sorry to say I can recall very little. The rustle of the water as it hissed against our stem, and the wind in the birches and junipers on the banks, soon lulled me. I was only awakened by the canoe touching the bank at Big Tree.

Big Tree Portage is a recognized camping-place, situated between the great main lumber-camp of Briston and Harpur and the settlement of St. Amiel, and it lies about equidistant from both. Old fire-scars in the clearing showed black not more than thirty yards from the water. From the canoe we were in full sight of the scene of the tragedy.

A small shelter of boughs stood beneath the spreading branches of a large fir; the ground all about was strewn with tins and debris. On a bare space in front of the shelter, beside the charred logs of a camp-fire, a patch of blue caught my eye. This, as my sight grew accustomed to the light, resolved itself into the shape of a huge man. He lay upon his face, and the wind fluttered the blue blouse which he was wearing. It came upon me with a shock that I was looking at the body of Henry Lyon, the murdered man.

November, standing up in the canoe, a wood picture in his buckskin shirt and jeans, surveyed the scene in silence, then pushed off again and paddled up and down, staring at the bank. After a bit he put in and waded ashore

In obedience to a sign I stayed in the canoe, from which I watched the movements of my companion. First, he went to the body and examined it with minute care; next, he disappeared within the shelter, came out, and stood for a minute staring towards the river; finally, he called to me to come ashore.

I had seen November turn the body over, and as I came up I was aware of a great ginger-bearded face, horribly pale, confronting the sky. It was easy to see how the man had died, for the bullet had torn a hole at the base of the neck. The ground beside him was torn up as if by some small sharp instruments.

The idea occurred to me that I would try my hand at detection. I went into the shelter. There I found a blanket, two freshly flayed bearskins, and a pack, which lay open. I came out again and carefully examined the ground in all directions. Suddenly looking up, I saw November Joe watching me with a kind of grim and covert amusement.

"What are you looking for?" said he.

"The tracks of the murderer."

"You won't find them."

"Why?"

"He didn't make none."

I pointed out the spot where the ground was torn.

"The lumberman that found him—spiked boots," said November.

"How do you know he was not the murderer?"

"He didn't get here till Lyon had been dead for hours. Compare his tracks with Lyon's . . . much fresher. No, Mr. Sport, that cock won't fight."

"Then, as you seem to know so much, tell me what you *do* know."

"I know that Lyon reached here in the afternoon of the day before yesterday. He'd been visiting his traps upstream. He hadn't been here more'n a few minutes, and was lighting his pipe in the shelter there, when he hears a voice hail him. He comes out and sees a man in a canoe shoved into the bank. That man shot him dead and cleared off—without leaving a trace."

"How can you be sure of all this?" I asked, for not one of these things had occurred to my mind.

"Because I found a pipe of tobacco not rightly lit, but just charred on top, beside Lyon's body, and a newly used match in this shack. The man that killed him come downstream and surprised him."

"How can you tell he came downstream?"

"Because, if he'd come upstream Lyon would 'a' seen him from the shack," said November with admirable patience.

"You say the shot was fired from a canoe?"

"The river's too wide to shoot across; and, anyway, there's the mark of where the canoe rested agin the bank. No, this is the work of a right smart woodsman, and he's not left me one clue as to who he is. But I'm not through with him, mister. Such men as he needs catching. . . . Let's boil the kettle."

We laid the dead man inside the shack, and then, coming out once more into the sunlight, sat down beside a fire which we built among the stones on the bank of the river. Here November made tea in true woods fashion, drawing all the strength and bitterness from the leaves by boiling them. . . . I was wondering what he would do next, for it appeared that our chance of catching the murderer was infinitesimal, since he had left no clue save the mark on the bank where his canoe had rested among the reeds while he fired his deadly bullet. I put my thoughts into words.

"You're right," said November. "When a chap who's used to the woods life takes to crime, he's harder to lay hands on than a lynx in a alder patch."

"There is one thing which I don't understand," said I. "Why did not the murderer sink Lyon's body in the water? It would have been well hidden there."

The young woodsman pointed to the river, which foamed in low rapids about dark heads of rock.

"He couldn't trust her; the current's sharp, and would put the dead man ashore as like as not," he replied. "And if he'd landed to carry it down to his canoe, he'd have left tracks. No, he's done his work to rights from his point of view."

I saw the force of the argument, and nodded.

"And more'n that, there's few people," he went on, "travel up and down this river. Lyon might 'a' laid in that clearing till he was a skeleton, but for the chance of that lumber-jack happening along."

"Then which way do you think the murderer has fled?"

"Can't say," said he, "and, anyhow, he's maybe eighty miles away by this."

"Will you try and follow him?"

"No, not yet. I must find out something about him first. But, look here, mister, there's one fact you haven't given much weight to. This shooting was *pre*-meditated. The murderer *knew* that Lyon would camp here. The chances are a hundred to one against their having met by accident. The chap that killed him followed him downstream. Now, suppose I can find Lyon's last camp, I may learn something more. It can't be very far off, for he had a tidy-sized pack to carry, besides those green skins, which loaded him a bit. . . . And, anyway, it's my only chance."

So we set out upon our walk. November soon picked up Lyon's trail, leading from Big Tree Portage to a disused tote-road, which again led us due west between the aisles of the forest. From midday on through the whole of the afternoon we travelled. Squirrels chattered and hissed at us from the spruces, hardwood partridges drummed in the clearings, and once a red-deer buck bounded across our path with its white flag waving and dipping as it was swallowed up in the sun-speckled orange and red of the woods.

Lyon's trail was, fortunately, easy to follow, and it was only where, at long intervals, paths from the north or south broke into the main logging-road that November had reason to pause. But one by one we passed these by, until at last the tracks we were following shot away among the trees, and after a mile of deadfalls and moss debouched into a little clearing beside a backwater grown round with high yellow grass, and covered over the larger part of its surface with lily-pads.

The trail, after leading along the margin of this water, struck back to a higher reach of the same river that ran by Big Tree Portage, and then we were at once on the site of the deserted camp.

The very first thing my eye lit upon caused me to cry out in excitement, for side by side were two beds of balsam branches, that had evidently been placed under the shelter of the same tent cover. November, then, was right, Lyon *had* camped with someone on the night before he died.

I called out to him. His quiet patience and an attitude as if rather detached from events fell away from him like a cloak, and with almost uncanny swiftness he was making his examination of the camp.

I entirely believe that he was unconscious of my presence, so concentrated was he on his work as I followed him from spot to spot with an interest and excitement that no form of big-game shooting has ever given me. Now, man was the quarry, and, as it seemed, a man more dangerous than any beast. But I was destined to disappointment, for, as far as I could see, Joe discovered neither clue nor anything unusual.

To begin with, he took up and sifted through the layers of balsam boughs which had composed the beds, but apparently made no find. From them he turned quickly to kneel down by the ashy remains of the fire, and to examine the charred logs one by one. After that he followed a well-marked trail that led away from the lake to a small marsh in the farther part of which masts of dead timber were standing in great profusion. Nearer at hand a number of stumps showed where the campers had chopped the wood for their fire.

After looking closely at these stumps, November went swiftly back to the camp and spent the next ten minutes in following the tracks which led in all directions. Then once more he came back to the fire and methodically lifted off one charred stick after another. At the time I could not imagine why he did this, but, when I understood it, the reason was as simple and obvious as was that of his every action when once it was explained.

Before men leave a camp they seem instinctively to throw such trifles as they do not require or wish to carry on with them in the fire, which is generally expiring, for a first axiom of the true camper in the woods is never to leave his fire alight behind him, in case of a chance ember starting a forest conflagration.

In this case November had taken off nearly every bit of wood before I heard him utter a smothered exclamation as he held up a piece of stick.

I took it into my own hands and looked it over. It was charred, but I saw that one end had been split and the other end sharpened.

"What in the world is it?" I asked, puzzled.

November smiled. "Just evidence," he answered.

I was glad he had at last found something to go upon, for, so far, the camp had appeared to produce parsimoniously little that was suggestive. Nevertheless, I did not see how this little bit of spruce, crudely fashioned and split as it was, would lead us very far.

November spent another few minutes in looking everything over a second time, then he took up his axe and split a couple of logs and lit the fire. Over it he hung his inevitable kettle and boiled up the leaves of our morning brew with a liberal handful freshly added.

"Well," I said, as he touched the end of a burning ember to his pipe, "has this camp helped you?"

"Some," said November. "And you?"

He put the question quite seriously, though I suspect not without some inward irony.

"I can see that two men slept under one tent cover, that they cut the wood for their fire in that marsh we visited, and that they were here for a day, perhaps two."

"One was here for three days, the other one night," corrected November.

"How can you tell that?"

November pointed to the ground at the far side of the fire.

"To begin with, number 1 had his camp pitched over there," said he; then, seeing my look of perplexity, he added pityingly: "We've a westerly wind these last two days, but before that the wind was east, and he camped the first night with his back to it. And in the new camp one bed o' boughs is fresher than the other."

The thing seemed so absurdly obvious that I was nettled.

"I suppose there are other indications I haven't noticed," I said.

"There might be some you haven't mentioned," he answered warily.

"What are they?"

"That the man who killed Lyon is thick-set and very strong; that he has been a good while in the woods without having gone to a settlement; that he owns a blunt hatchet such as we woods chaps call 'tomahawk, number 3'; that he killed a moose last week; that he can read; that he spent the night before the murder in great trouble of mind, and that likely he was a religious kind o' chap."

As November reeled off these details in his quiet, low-keyed voice, I stared at him in amazement.

"But how can you have found out all that?" I said at last. "If it's correct, it's wonderful!"

"I'll tell you, if you still want to hear, when I've got my man—if ever I do get him. One thing more is sure, he is a chap who knew Lyon well. The rest of the job lies in the settlement of St. Amiel, where Lyon lived."

We walked back to Big Tree Portage, and from there ran down in the canoe to St. Amiel, arriving the following evening. About half a mile short of the settlement, November landed and set up our camp. Afterwards we went on. I had never before visited the place, and I found it to be a little colony of scattered houses, straggling beside the river. It possessed two stores and one of the smallest churches I have ever seen.

"You can help me here if you will," said November as we paused before the larger of the stores.

"Of course I will. How?"

"By letting 'em think you've engaged me as your guide and we've come in to St. Amiel to buy some grub and gear we've run short of."

"All right." And with this arrangement we entered the store.

I will not make any attempt to describe by what roundabout courses of talk November learned all the news of desolate little St. Amiel and of the surrounding countryside. Had I not known exactly what he wanted, I should never have dreamed that he was seeking information. He played the desultory uninterested listener to perfection. The Provincial Police had evidently found means to close the mouth of the lumber-jack for the time, at least, as no hint of Lyon's death had yet drifted back to his native place.

Little by little it came out that only five men were absent from the settlement. Two of these, Fitz and Baxter Gurd, were brothers who had gone on an extended trapping expedition. The other absentees were Highamson, Lyon's father-in-law; Thomas Miller, a professional guide and hunter; and, lastly, Henry Lyon himself, who had gone up-river to visit his traps, starting on the previous Friday. The other men had all been away three weeks or more, and all had started in canoes, except Lyon, who, having sold his, went on foot.

Next, by imperceptible degrees, the talk slid round to the subject of Lyon's wife. They had been married four years and had no child. She had been the belle of St. Amiel, and there had been no small competition for her hand. Of the absent men, both Miller and Fitz Gurd had been her suitors, and the former and Lyon had never been on good terms since the marriage. The younger Gurd was a wild fellow, and only his brother's influence kept him straight.

So much we heard before November wrapped up our purchases and we took our leave.

No sooner were we away than I put my eager question: "What do you think of it?"

Joe shrugged his shoulders.

"Do you know any of these men?"

"All of them."

"How about the fellow who is on bad terms with—"

November seized my arm. A man was approaching through the dusk. As he passed, my companion hailed him.

"Hullo, Baxter! Didn't know you'd come back. Where you been?"

"Right up on the headwaters."

"Fitz come down with you?"

"No; stayed on the line of traps. Did you want him, November?"

"Yes, but it can wait. See any moose?"

"Nary one—nothing but red deer."

"Good-night."

"So long."

"That settles it," said November. "If he speaks the truth, as I believe he does, it wasn't either of the Gurds shot Lyon."

"Why not?"

"Didn't you hear him say they hadn't seen any moose? And I told you that the man that shot Lyon had killed a moose quite recent. That leaves just Miller and Highamson—and it weren't Miller."

"You're sure of that?"

"Stark certain. One reason is that Miller's above six foot, and the man as camped with Lyon wasn't as tall by six inches. Another reason. You heard the storekeeper say how Miller and Lyon wasn't on speaking terms; yet the man who shot Lyon camped with him— slep' beside him — must 'a' talked to him. That weren't Miller."

His clear reasoning rang true.

"Highamson lives alone away up above Lyon's," continued November; "he'll make back home soon."

"Unless he's guilty and has fled the country," I suggested.

"He won't 'a' done that. It 'ud be as good as a confession. No, he thinks he's done his work to rights and has nothing to fear. Like as not he's back home now. There's not much coming and going between these up-river places and St. Amiel, and he might easy be there and no one know it yet down to the settlement. We'll go up to-night and make sure. But first we'll get back to camp and take a cup o' tea."

The night had become both wild and blustering before we set out for Highamson's hut, and all along the forest paths which led to it the sleet and snow of what November called "a real mean night" beat in our faces.

As we travelled on in silence, my mind kept going over and over the events of the last two days. I had already seen enough to assure me that my companion was a very skilful detective, but the most ingenious part of his work, namely, the deductions by which he had pretended to reconstruct the personality of the criminal, had yet to be put to the test.

It was black dark, or nearly so, when at last a building loomed up in front of us, a faint light showing under the door.

"You there, Highamson?" called out November.

As there was no answer, my companion pushed it open and we entered the small wooden room, where, on a single table, a lamp burned dimly. He turned it up and looked around. A pack lay on the floor unopened, and a gun leant up in a corner.

"Just got in," commented November. "Hasn't loosed up his pack yet."

He turned it over. A hatchet was thrust through the wide thongs which bound it. November drew it out.

"Put your thumb along that edge," he said. "Blunt? Yes? Yet he drove that old hatchet as deep in the wood as Lyon drove his sharp one: he's a strong man."

As he spoke he was busying himself with the pack, examining its contents with deft fingers. It held little save a few clothes, a little tea and salt, and other fragments of provisions, and a Bible. The finding of the last was, I could see, no surprise to November, though the reason why he should have suspected its presence remained hidden from me. But I had begun to realize that much was plain to him which to the ordinary man was invisible.

Having satisfied himself as to every article in the pack, he rapidly replaced them, and tied it up as he had found it, when I, glancing out of the small window, saw a light moving low among the trees, to which I called November Joe's attention.

"It's likely Highamson," he said, "coming home with a lantern. Get you into that dark corner."

I did so, while November stood in the shadow at the back of the closed door. From my position I could see the lantern slowly approaching until it flung a gleam of light through the window into the hut. The next moment the door was thrust open, and the heavy breathing of a man became audible.

It happened that at first Highamson saw neither of us, so that the first intimation that he had of our presence was November's "Hello!"

Down crashed the lantern, and its bearer started back with a quick hoarse gasp.

"Who's there?" he cried, "who—"

"Them as is sent by Hal Lyon."

Never have I seen words produce so tremendous an effect.

Highamson gave a bellow of fury, and the next instant he and November were struggling together.

I sprang to my companion's aid, and even then it was no easy task for the two of us to master the powerful old man. As we held him down I caught my first sight of his ash-grey face. His mouth grinned open, and there was a terrible intention in his staring eyes. But all changed as he recognized his visitor.

"November! November Joe!" cried he.

"Get up!" And as Highamson rose to his feet, "Whatever for did you do it?" asked November in his quiet voice. But now its quietness carried a menace.

"Do what? I didn't'—I—" Highamson paused, and there was something unquestionably fine about the old man as he added: "No, I won't lie. It's true I shot Hal Lyon. And, what's more, if it was to do again, I'd do it again! It's the best deed I ever done; yes, I say that, though I know it's written in the book: 'Whoso sheddeth man's blood, by man shall his blood be shed.'"

"Why did you do it?" repeated November.

Highamson gave him a look.

"I'll tell you. I did it for my little Janey's sake. He was her husband. See here! I'll tell you why I shot Hal Lyon. Along of the first week of last month I went away back into the woods trapping muskrats. I was gone more'n the month, and the day I come back I did as I did to-night, as I always do first thing when I gets in—I went over to see Janey. Hal Lyon weren't there; if he had been, I shouldn't never 'a' needed to travel so far to get even with him. But that's neither here nor there. He'd gone to his bear traps above Big Tree; but the night before he left he'd got in one of his quarrels with my Janey. Hit her—he did—there was one tooth gone where his—fist fell."

Never have I seen such fury as burned in the old man's eyes as he groaned out the last words.

"Janey, that had the prettiest face for fifty miles around. She tried to hide it from me,—she didn't want me to know,—but there was her poor face all swole, and black and blue, and the gap among her white teeth. Bit by bit it all came out. It weren't the first time Lyon'd took his hands to her, no, nor the third, nor the fourth. There on the spot, as I looked at her, I made up my mind I'd go after him, and I'd make him promise me, aye, swear to me, on the Holy Book, never to lay hand on her again. If he wouldn't swear I'd put him where his hands couldn't reach her. I found him camped away up alongside a backwater near his traps, and I told him I'd seen Janey and that he must swear. . . . He wouldn't! He said he'd learn her to tell on him, he'd smash her in the mouth again. Then he lay down and slep'. I wonder now he weren't afraid of me, but I suppose that was along of me being a quiet, God-fearing chap. . . . Hour by hour I lay awake, and then I couldn't stand it no more, and I got up and pulled a bit of candle I had from my pack, fixed up a candlestick, and looked in my Bible for guidance. And the words I lit on were: 'Thou shalt break them with a rod of iron.' That was the gun clear enough. . . . Then I blew out the light, and I think I slep', for I dreamed.

"Next morning Lyon was up early. He had two or three green skins that he'd took off the day before, and he said he was going straight home to smash Janey. I lay there and I said nothing, black nor white. His judgment was set. I knew he couldn't make all the distance in one day, and I was pretty sure he'd camp at Big Tree. I arrived there just after him, as I could travel faster by canoe than him walking, and so kep' near him all day. It was nigh sunset, and I bent down under the bank so he couldn't see me. He went into the old shack. I called out his name. I heard him cursing at my voice, and when he showed his face I shot him dead. I never landed, I never left no tracks, I thought I was safe, sure. You've took me; yet only for Janey's sake I wouldn't care. I did right, but she won't like them to say her father's a murderer. . . . That's all."

November sat on the edge of the table. His handsome face was grave. Nothing more was said for a good while. Then Highamson stood up.

"I'm ready, November, but you'll let me see Janey again before you give me over to the police."

November looked him in the eyes. "Expect you'll see a good deal of Janey yet. She'll be lonesome over there now that her brute husband's gone. She'll want you to live with her," he said.

"D'ye mean . . ."

November nodded. "If the police can catch you for themselves, let 'em. And you'd lessen the chance of that a wonderful deal if you was to burn them moose-shank moccasins you're wearing. When did you kill your moose?"

"Tuesday's a week. And my moccasins was wore out, so I fixed 'em up woods fashion."

"I know. The hair on 'em is slipping. I found some of it in your tracks in the camp, away above Big Tree. That's how I knew you'd killed a moose. I found your candlestick too. Here it is." He took from his pocket the little piece of spruce stick, which had puzzled me so much, and turned towards me.

"This end's sharp to stick into the earth, that end's slit and you fix the candle in with a bit o' birch bark. Now it can go into the stove along o' the moccasins." He opened the stove door and thrust in the articles.

"Only three know your secret, Highamson, and if I was you I wouldn't make it four, not even by adding a woman to it."

Highamson held out his hand.

"You always was a white man, Nov," said he.

Hours later, as we sat drinking a final cup of tea at the camp-fire, I said:—

"After you examined Lyon's upper camp, you told me seven things about the murderer. You've explained how you knew them, all but three."

"What are the three?"

"First, how did you know that Highamson had been a long time in the woods without visiting a settlement?"

"His moccasins was wore out and patched with raw moose-hide. The tracks of them was plain," replied November.

I nodded. "And how could you tell that he was religious and spent the night in great trouble of mind?"

November paused in filling his pipe. "He couldn't sleep," said he, "and so he got up and cut that candlestick. What'd he want to light a candle for but to read by? And why should he want to read in the middle of the night if he was not in trouble? And if he was in trouble, what book would he want to read? Besides, not one trap-per in a hundred carries any book but the Bible."

"I see. But how did you know it was in the middle of the night?"

"Did you notice where he cut his candlestick?"

"No," said I.

"I did, and he made two false cuts where his knife slipped in the dark. You're wonderful at questions."

"And you at answers."

November stirred the embers under the kettle, and the firelight lit up his fine face as he turned with a yawn.

"My!" said he, "but I'm glad Highamson had his reasons. I'd 'a' hated to think of that old man shut in where he couldn't see the sun rise. Wouldn't you?"

4

THE SEVEN LUMBER-JACKS

The more I saw of Joe in the days which followed, the more I appreciated the man and the more I became convinced of his remarkable gifts. Indeed, truth to tell, I could not restrain the hope that some new situation might arise which would give him an opportunity of displaying them once again. Of course, the ordinary details of our woods life provided him with some scope, and it was always a pleasure to me to be in the company of so consummate a woodsman. It was not long after our return from St. Amiel before Joe succeeded in getting me a fair shot at the large red-deer buck of Widdeney Pond, and it so happened that the killing of this buck brought us news of old Highamson, for we took the head down to him to set up, since Joe assured me that the old man had once worked with success at a taxidermist's.

Joe and I walked over and found him living with his daughter, Janey Lyon, for the police had never been successful in discovering the identity of the avenger of Big Tree Portage. The two seemed very happy together, but I must acknowledge that I feared from what I saw that the beautiful Janey would not continue to bear the name of Lyon much longer. I said as much to November Joe as we were walking back.

"That's nature," said he. "Old man Highamson told me that neither Baxter Gurd nor Miller don't give her no peace. Well, I guess a woman's better married anyway."

"How about a man, Joe?" I asked.

34

"It maybe all right for them as don't get the pull o' the woods too strong, but for him that's heard the loons calling on the lakes, 't is different someway."

"Yet there are some very pretty girls, Joe."

"You've seen more than I have, Mr. Quaritch," said Joe, laughingly; "but you don't get no telegrams from Mrs. Quaritch telling you to come home and sing to baby."

To this too trenchant remark I could think of no immediate reply, and we continued our way for some time in silence. It was drawing on towards evening and had begun to rain when we turned from the woods into the mile-long trail that led to November's shack. His quick glance fell at once upon the ground, and following his eye, I saw the impression of fresh tracks.

"What do they tell you?" I asked, for it was always a matter of interest to me to put November's skill to the little daily tests that came in my way.

"Try yourself," said he.

They were ordinary tracks, and, look as I would, I could not glean much information from them.

"A man in moccasins—probably an Indian —has passed along. Isn't that right?" I asked.

November Joe smiled grimly.

"Not just quite. The man isn't an Indian; he's a white man, and he carries big news, and has not come very far."

"You're sure?" I said, stooping to examine the trail more closely, but without result.

"Certain! The Indian moccasin has no raised heel. These have. He's not come far; he's travelling fast—see, he springs from the ball of the foot; and when a man finishes a journey on the run, you may be sure he thinks he's got a good reason for getting to the end of it. This trail leads nowhere but to my shack, and we'll sure find our man there."

Ten minutes later, when we came in sight of November's home, we were aware of a big man sitting on a log smoking his pipe beside the door. He was middle-aged, with a hard face, and there was more grey in his russet beard than his age warranted. As soon as we appeared he leaped up and came across the open to meet us.

"Blackmask is at it again!" he cried.

I saw a gleam of anticipation, if not of pleasure, cross November's face. He turned to me.

"This is Mr. Close, manager of the River Star Pulp Company's Camp C," he said. "I'd like to make you known to Mr. Quaritch, Mr. Close." This courtesy concluded, he added in his deliberate tones, "What's Blackmask done now?"

"He's at his old tricks! But this year we'll lay him by the heels, or my name's not Joshua Close." The speaker looked up, and, seeing my puzzled expression, addressed himself to me.

"Last year there were five separate robberies committed on the road between Camp C and the settlement," he explained. "Each time it was just a single lumber-jack who got held up, and each time a man in a black mask was the robber. November here was away."

"Up in Wyoming with a Philadelphia lawyer after elk," supplemented the tall young woodsman.

"The police failed to make any arrest, though once they were on the ground within four hours of the hold-up," went on Close. "But all that is ancient history. It is what happened to Dan Michaels last night that brought me here at seven miles an hour. Dan has been working for pretty nigh a three months' stretch, and the day before yesterday he came into the office and told me his mother was dead, and he must have leave for the funeral. Dan's a good man, and I tried to dissuade him, and reminded him that he had buried his mother the last time when we were up on the lakes not a year ago. But it wasn't any use; he'd got the fever on him, and he wouldn't listen. He had a good big roll of bills due, and I could see he meant to blow them, so I paid him, and told him I'd try to keep a job warm for him till he came back from the funeral. I gave him ten days to get through with his spree. Well, it was along about four o'clock when I paid him off, and I made no doubt he'd sleep the night in the camp and get away at dawn; but that is just what he didn't do. Something I'd said annoyed him, and after telling the cook his opinion of me, and saying he wouldn't sleep another night in a camp where I was boss, he legged out for the settlement."

"By himself?"

"Yes, alone. Next morning, bright and early, he was back again, and this was the yarn he slung me. . . . He'd made about eight miles when it came on darkish, and he decided to camp just beyond where we did the most of our timber cut last year. The night was fine, and he had only his turkey (bundle) and a blanket with him, so he went to the side of the trail at Perkins's Clearing, and lay down beside a fire which he built against a rock with spruces behind it. He slept at once, and remembers nothing more until he was started awake by a voice shouting at him. He sat up blinking, but the talk he heard soon fetched his eyes open.

"'Hands up, and no fooling!'

"Of course, he put up his hands; he'd no choice, for he couldn't see anyone. Then another man who was in the bushes behind his back ordered him to haul out his bundle of notes and chuck them to the far side of the fire, or take the consequences. Dan saw a revolver barrel gleam in the bush. He cursed a bit, but the thieves had the drop on him, so he just had to out with his wad of notes and heave them over as he was told. A birch log in the fire flared up at the minute, and as the notes touched the ground he saw a chap in a black mask step out and pick them up, and then jump back into the dark. All the time Dan had one eye on the revolver of the man in the bushes. It kept him covered, so he had no show. Then the voice that spoke first gave him the hint not to move for two hours, or he'd be shot like a dog. He sat out the two hours by his watch without hearing a sound, and then came back to C.

"When the boys got the facts, the whole camp was nigh as mad as he was. They put up fifty dollars' reward for anyone giving information that will lead to catching the robbers, and I added another hundred for the Company. So now, Joe, if you can clap your hand on the brutes you'll be doing yourself a good turn and others too."

Close ended his narration, and looked at November, who had listened throughout in his habitual silence.

"Do the boys up at C know you've come to me?" he said.

"No, I thought it wiser they shouldn't."

November remained silent for a moment.

"You'd best get away back, Mr. Close," he said at length. "I'll go down to Perkins's Clearing, and have a look at the spot where the robbery took place, and then I'll find some excuse to take me to Camp C, when I can make my report to you."

To this Close agreed, and soon we saw him striding away until his strong figure was swallowed up in the forest twilight.

On his departure I tried to talk to November about the robbery, but never have I found him less communicative. He sat with his pipe in his teeth and kept on turning our conversation to other topics until the two of us set out through the woods.

The moon, as it swept across the arc of the sky, guided us upon our way, which, after the first short cut along an immense hardwood ridge, was good travelling enough. So we journeyed until, just as the trees became a gigantic etching in black against the grey dawn-lights, we came suddenly out into the open of the clearing.

"This is the place," said November.

As soon as the light strengthened, he examined the site of Dan Michaels's bivouac. The ashes of a fire and a few boughs made its scanty furnishings, and in neither did November take much interest. Forth and back he moved, apparently following lines of tracks which the drenching rain of the previous day had almost obliterated, until, indeed, after ten minutes, he gave it up.

"Well, well," said he, in his soft-cadenced voice, "he always did have the luck."

"Who?"

"The robber. Look at last year! Got clear every time!"

"The robbers," I corrected.

"There's but one," said he.

"Michaels mentioned two voices; and the man in the mask stepped into sight at the same moment as the fire glinted on the revolver of the other man in the bushes."

Without a word November led me to the farther side of the dead fire and parted the boughs of a spruce, which I had previously seen him examine. At a height of less than five feet from the ground one or two twigs were broken, and the bark had been rubbed near the trunk.

"He was a mighty interesting man, him with the revolver." November threw back his handsome head and laughed. "There was only one chap, and he fixed the revolver here in that fork. It was a good bluff he played on Dan, making him think there was two agin' him! . . . The rain's washed out most of the tracks, so we'll go up to Camp C and try our luck there. But first I'd best shoot a deer, and the boys'll think I only come to carry them some meat, as I often do when I kill anywhere nigh the camp."

As we made our way towards C, November found the tracks of a young buck which had crossed the tote-road since the rain, and while I waited he slipped away like a shadow into the wild raspberry growth, returning twenty minutes later with the buck upon his shoulders. As a hunter and a quiet mover in the woods, November can rarely have been surpassed.

On reaching Camp C, November sold his deer to the cook, and then we went to the office. The men were all away at work but we found the manager, to whom November told his news. I noticed, however, he said nothing of his idea that there had been but one robber.

"That just spells total failure," remarked Close when he had finished.

November assented. "Guess we'll have to wait till another chap is held up," said he.

"You think they'll try their hand at it again?"

"Sure. Who'd stop after such success?"

"I'd be inclined to agree with you, if it wasn't for the fact that the men won't leave singly now. They're scared to. A party of six started this afternoon. They were hoping they'd have the luck to meet the scoundrels, and bucking how they'd let daylight into them if they did. But of course they won't turn up—they'd be shy of such a big party!"

"Maybe," said November. "With your permission, Mr. Close, me and Mr. Quaritch'll sleep here to-night."

"All right. But I can't attend to you. I'm behind with my accounts, and I must even them up if it takes all night."

"And there's one question I'd like to have an answer to. It's just this. How did the robber *know* that Dan Michaels was worth holding up? Or that he was going off on the spree? He must have been told by some one. Blackmask has got a friend in Camp C all right. That is, unless—"

"Aye, unless?" repeated the manager.

But November would say no more. An idea had come into his mind, but Close could not draw it from him; yet I could see he had entire trust in the taciturn young woodsman.

Next morning November seemed in no hurry to go, and shortly before the midday meal a party of half a dozen men rushed into the camp. They were all shouting at once, and it was impossible for a time to discover what the turmoil was about. The manager came out to hear what they had to say. The cook and the cookee had joined themselves to the group, and they, too, were talking and gesticulating with extraordinary freedom.

Leaning against the wall of the bunkhouse, the silent November surveyed the clamouring knot of men with grim humour.

"I tell you again, we've been held up, robbed, cleaned out, the whole six of us!" yelled a short man with a sandy beard.

"Thot is true," cried a fair-haired Swede.

On this they all began shouting again, waving their arms and explaining. November advanced. "Look, boys, that's an easy, comfortable log over there!"

The Swede answered him with a snarl, but meeting November's eyes thought better of it. Joe was the last person upon whom any one would choose to fix a quarrel.

"I was suggesting, boys," continued November, "that there's the log handy, and if you'd each choose a soft spot and leave one to speak and the others listen till he's through with it, we'd get at the facts. Every minute wasted gives them as robbed you the chance to get off clear."

"November's right," said a huge lumberman called Thompson. "Here's what happened. We six got our time yesterday morning, and after dinner we started off together. It were coming along dark when we camped in the old log hut of Tideson's Bridge. Seein' what had happened to Dan, we agreed to keep a watch till dawn. First watch was Harry's. In an hour and a half he were to wake me. He never did. . . . The sun were up before I woke, and there was all the others sleeping round me. I was wonderful surprised, but I took the kettle and was going down to fill her at the brook. It was then that I noticed my roll of bills was gone from my belt. I came running back. Harry woke, and when I told him, he clutches at his belt and finds his money gone, too. Then Chris, Bill Maver, Wedding Charlie, and last of all Long Lars, they wakes up and danged if the lot of them hadn't been robbed same as us."

A unanimous groan verified the statement. "We was tearing mad," went on the spokesman. "Then out we goes to search for the tracks of the thieves."

A look of despair crossed November's face. I knew he was thinking of the invaluable information the feet of the six victims must have blotted out forever.

"You found them?" inquired November.

"We did. They was plain enough," replied the big lumberman. "One man done it. He come up from the brook, did his business, and went back to the water. He was a big, heavy chap with large feet, and he wore tanned cowhide boots, patched on the right foot. There were seventeen nails in the heel of the right boot, and fifteen in the other. How's that for tracking?"

There was no doubt about the fact that November was surprised. He said nothing for a full minute, then he looked up sharply.

"How many bottles of whiskey had you?" said he.

"Nary one," answered Thompson. "There isn't one nearer than Lavallotte, as you well know. We wasn't drunk, we was drugged! We must 'a' been, though how it was done beats me, for we had nothing but bread and bacon and tea, and I made the tea myself."

"Where's the kettle?"

"We left that and the frying-pan back at the hut, for we're going to hunt the country for the thief. You'll come along, Nov?"

"On my own condition—or I'll have nothing to do with it!"

"What's it?"

"That nary a man of you goes back to Tideson's Bridge hut till I give you leave."

"But we want to catch the robber."

"Very well. Go and try if you think you can do it."

An outburst of argument arose, but soon one and another began to say, "We'll leave it to you, Nov."— "Mind you fetch my hundred and ninety dollars back for me, Nov."— "Leave Nov alone."— "Go on, Nov."

November laughed. "I suppose you all slept with your money on you?"

It appeared they all had, and Lars and Chris, who possessed pocketbooks, had found them flung empty in a corner of the hut.

"Well, Mr. Quaritch and me'll be getting along, boys. I'll let you know if I've any luck." Then suddenly November turned to the big spokesman and said: "By the way, Thompson, did you fill that kettle at the brook *before* you found you'd lost your cash?"

"No, I run right back."

"That's lucky," said November, and we walked away in a roar of shouted questions to the canoe placed at our disposal by Close. By water we could run down to Tideson's Bridge in an hour or two. It was plain November did not desire to talk, for as he plied the canoe-pole he sang, lifting his untrained but pathetic tenor in some of the most mournful songs I have ever heard. I learned later that sentimental pathos in music was highly approved by November. And many woodsmen are like him in that.

We slid on past groves of birch and thickets of alder, and presently I put a question,

"Do you think this is the work of the same man that held up Dan Michaels?"

"Guess so; can't be sure. The ground's fine and soft, and we ought to get the answer to a good many questions down there."

Thanks to the canoe and a short cut known to November, we arrived at our destination in admirable time. Tideson's Brook was a tributary of the river, and the bridge a rough affair of logs thrown over its shallow waters where it cut across the logging road. The hut, which had been the scene of the robbery, stood about a hundred yards from the north bank of the brook, a defined path leading down from it to the water.

First of all skirting the path, we went to the hut where the six had slept. A few articles dropped from the hastily made packs lay about, the frying-pan beside the stove, and the kettle on its side by the door. November moved round examining everything in his deft, light way; lastly, he picked up the kettle and peered inside.

"What's in it?" said I.

"Nothing," returned November.

"Well, Thompson told you he hadn't filled it," I reminded him.

He gave me a queer little smile. "Just so," said he, and strolled for fifty yards or so up the tote-road.

"I've been along looking at the footmarks of them six moss-backs," he volunteered; "now we'll look around here."

The inspection of the tracks was naturally a somewhat lengthy business. November had studied the trail of the six men to some purpose, for though he hardly paused as he ranged the trodden ground, so swift were his eyes that he named each of the men to me as he pointed to their several tracks. As we approached the bank, he indicated a distinct set of footsteps, which we followed to the hut and back again to the water.

"He's the chap that did it," said November. "That's pretty plain. What do you say about him?" he turned to me.

"He is a heavier man than I am, and he walks rather on his heels."

November nodded, and began to follow the trail, which went down into the stream. He stood at the water's edge examining some stones which had been recently displaced, then waded down into it.

"Where was his boat?" I asked.

But November had by now reached a large flat stone some feet out in the water, and this he was looking round and over with great care. Then he beckoned to me. The stone was a large flat one, as I have said, and he showed me some scratches upon its farther surface. The scratches were deep and irregular. I stared at them, but to me they conveyed nothing.

"They don't look like the mark of a boat," I ventured.

"They aren't. But that chap made them all right," he said.

"But how or why?"

November laughed. "I won't answer that yet. But I'll tell you this. The robbery was done between two and three o'clock last night."

"What makes you say that?"

November pointed to a grove of birch on the nearer bank.

"Those trees," he answered; then, on seeing my look of bewilderment, he added, "and he wasn't a two hundred pound man an' heavier than you, but a little thin chap, and he hadn't a boat."

"Then how did he get away? By wading?"

"Maybe he waded."

"If he did, he must have left the stream somewhere," I exclaimed.

"Sure."

"Then you'll be able to find his tracks where he landed."

"No need to."

"Why?"

"Because I'm sure of my man."

I could not repress the useless question. "But!" I cried in surprise, "who is he?"

"You'll see."

"Is it the same who held up Dan Michaels?"

"Yes."

With that I had to be satisfied. It was late at night when we approached Camp C. The hastening river showed dark brown and white as November poled the canoe onwards, and the roaring of the rapids was in our ears. But as we came along the quiet reach below the camp, we heard a great clamour and commotion. We jumped ashore and went silently straight to the office, where the manager lived. A crowd stood round, and two men were holding the door; one was the burly Thompson.

"Hello! You needn't bother no more, Nov," he shouted. "We've got him."

"Who've you got?"

"The blackguard that robbed us."

"Good!" said November. "Who is it?"

"Look at him!" Thompson banged open the office door and showed us the manager, Close, sitting on a chair by the fire, looking a good deal dishevelled.

"Mr. Close?" exclaimed November.

"Yes, the boss—no other!"

"Got evidence?" inquired November, staring at Close.

"Tiptop! No one seen him from dark to dawn. And we got the boots. Found 'em in a biscuit-tin on a shelf in the shanty just behind here where he sleeps."

"You fool! I was at my accounts all night!" cried Close to Thompson.

November took no notice.

"Who found the boots?" said he.

"Cookee, when he was cleaning up. Found a bottle of sleeping-stuff, too—near empty," shouted two or three together.

November whistled. "Good for cookee. Has he owned up?" he nodded at Close. "Was they your boots, Mr. Close?"

"Yes," roared Close.

November looked back at the lumbermen with a meaning eye.

"But he denies the robbery!" said Thompson excitedly.

"Of course I deny it!" cried Close.

"Let's see them boots," put in November.

"The boys took 'em to the bunkhouse," said Thompson. "Say, Nov, think of him paying us with one hand and robbing us with the other, the—"

"Wonderful!" observed November in his dry way. He continued to stare hard at Close, who at last looked up, and I could have sworn I saw November Joe's dark-lashed eyelid droop slightly in his direction.

A change came over the manager. "Get out of here," he cried angrily. "Get out of here, you and your woods detective!" and some uncommonly warm language charged out at the back of the closing door.

In the bunkhouse, where we found a score and a half of lumber-jacks smoking and talking, November was received hilariously, and some witticisms were indulged in at his expense; but they soon died a natural death, and the boots were produced.

The men who had been robbed and their comrades closed round as November examined them.

"Seventeen in one heel and fifteen in the other—cowhide boots," said Chris, "that's what he that robbed us wore, and I'll swear to that."

"I could swear to it, too," agreed November.

"Take them *and* the sleeping-stuff," pursued Chris; "it's a silver fox skin to a red on a conviction, eh, November?"

"Have you sent for the police?"

"Not yet. We'd waited till you come up. We'll send now."

"The sooner the better," said November. "And whoever goes'll find four chaps from Camp B in the hut by Tideson's Bridge. They've orders to knock it down and take the roof off and carry the stove into D."

I listened to November making this astonishing statement, and hoped I showed no surprise.

What on earth was the game that he was playing?

"Hurry up, boys, and send for the police, or there may be trouble. Who's going?"

"I don't mind if I go," offered Chris. "I'll start right now. The sooner we get Mr.—Close safe in gaol, the better."

We all saw Chris off, and then the men took us back into the bunkhouse, where they talked and argued for an hour. November had relapsed into his usual taciturnity. But when at length he spoke again his words acted like a bombshell.

"Say, boys," he said, and the cadence of his accent was very marked, "it's about time we let the boss out."

Every head jerked round in his direction. "Let him out?" shouted a dozen voices. "Before the police come?"

"Best so," replied November in his gentle manner. "You see, it wasn't him held you up, boys."

"Who was it, then?"

November stood up.

"Come, and I'll show you."

Finally four of us boarded the big canoe and set off. They were Thompson, Wedding Charlie, November, and myself. It was a memorable voyage. November stood in the stern, Wedding Charlie in the bows, while Thompson and I sat between with nothing to do. Our craft rushed down through the creaming rapids, the banks flashed by, and in an astonishingly short space of time we had left the canoe and were walking through the woods.

I lost all sense of direction in the darkness until we came out on the banks of the brook near Tideson's Bridge. We crossed, and all four of us crouched in the shadow of a big rock not twenty yards from the hut. We had been forewarned by November to keep very quiet and to watch the hut.

It seemed to me that hours went by while I stared at the shifting moonlight and the creeping shadows. Dimly I foresaw what was about to happen. The pale forelights of dawn were already in the air when I felt November move slightly, and a moment later I heard a stick break, then footfalls on the bridge. A bluish shadow came cautiously down the bank, hesitating at every step, but always approaching the hut, until at last it passed within it. Then a match flared inside; I saw it pass the broken window. There was a pause; the door creaked faintly and the figure stole out again.

I put out my hands towards November—he was gone.

Meantime the figure from the hut was moving up the path to the road, and a second figure was gaining on him. I recognized November's mighty outlines as he followed with arms outstretched. Then the arms fell, and there was a cry, almost a shriek.

When we ran up, November was holding Chris struggling on the ground.

"Search him, boys," said November. "He's got the stuff on him."

Thompson's big hand dived into the breast of Chris's shirt and when it came out again it held a bundle of notes.

"You smart cuss!" said Chris to November Joe.

A few busy hours followed and it was the next afternoon before I found myself again at November's shanty and asked for the explanations which had been promised me.

"The moment I heard Thompson's story," began November, "it started me thinking a bit. You remember how plain they saw the tracks of the robber, the size, the patch, the exact number of nails. It sort of seemed that a road agent who went around in a pair of boots like that was maybe a fool, or maybe laying a false trail."

"I see," said I.

"As soon as I saw the tracks, I knew I wasn't far out as to the false trail. The chap wanted the tracks seen; he walked more'n once on the soft ground a purpose."

"Then he wasn't a heavy man, anyway," I put in. "You thought—"

"How did I know he was a light man? Well, you saw those stones I showed you? He put them in a pack or something, and carried 'em to make them heavy tracks. I guessed from the set-out one of them six had done it."

"But how?"

"See, here's the way of it. I suspicioned some one in C from Dan Michaels's case. And look at those five hold-ups last year. Each one was done within ten miles of C. That showed me that the robber, whoever he was, couldn't operate far from camp. Then the drugging settled it. Don't you remember the kettle had nothing in it?"

I would have spoken, but November held up his hand.

"No, I know Thompson hadn't filled it, but he hadn't cleaned it either. We woods chaps always leave the tea-leaves in the kettle till we want to boil up the next brew. So it looked queer that some one had washed out that kettle. Now, if the robber come from outside he'd never do that, no need to. He'd be gone afore they could suspect the kettle. No, that clean kettle said plain as speaking that it was one of the six.

"Now," went on November, "when I knew that, I knew a good bit, and when I saw the scratches on the rock, I was able to settle up the whole caboodle—Chris put that stuff in the tea, and as soon as it sent them off asleep, he picked the money off them. Then he went down to the brook, taking the kettle, the big boots, and something to hold a pack of stones with him. He waded out to that flat rock and washed out the kettle, then he filled up his pack with stones and put on the boss's big boots. After that, he had no more to do but to walk up to the hut and back again, laying the false trail. After that he waded out to the rock again, so as to leave no tracks, and changed back into his own moccasins, went to the hut, and to sleep."

"But the scratches on the rock? What made them?"

"The nails in the boots. Chris drew up his feet to fasten up the boots, and the nails slipped a bit on the rock."

"But the time, November. You said the robbery was done between two and three in the morning. How did you know that?"

"By the birches. He'd turn to the light to put on his boots, and the moon only rose above them trees about two. Till then that side of the rock was in black shadow."

"And the stones in the pack?"

"The heel-tracks was good and marked. You yourself noticed how the chap walked on his heels?"

"Yes."

"That told me. A man with a weight upon his back always does it. And when I saw the stones that had been raked up out of the riverbed, why, there it was like print and plainer—that the robber was a light man. That got me as far as to know it was one of two men did it. Chris and Bill Mavers isn't sizeable, either of them; they're smallish made. It were one or other, I knew. Then, whichever it was, after he got the money, what did he do with it?"

"Took it with him or hid it," said I, as November seemed to expect a reply.

"When I comes to think it over, I was pretty sure he hid it. Cos if there'd happened to be any argument or quarrel or trouble about it there might 'a' been a search, and if the notes had 'a' been found on one of them, they'd have dropped him, sure. Next point was, where did he hide it? There was the rocks and the riverbank and the hut. But it was all notes, therefore the place'd have to be dry; so I pitches on the hut. That was right, Mr. Quaritch?"

"I couldn't have guessed better myself," I said, smiling.

November nodded. "So up we goes to C, and there we finds them mossbacks accusing the boss. Chris put the boots back in the shack and the bottle on the shelf. An old grudge made him do it. But I couldn't tell which of the two small chaps it was at that time. So I set the trap about the lumbermen breaking up the hut, and Chris walks into that. He knew if the hut was took down, the notes 'ud be found. You'd think the ground was hot under him until he starts to bring the police—and him the laziest fellow in C! The minute he offered to go, I knew I had him."

"And you still think Chris robbed Dan?"

"I know it. There was a hundred and twenty-seven dollars that can't be accounted for in the bundle we took off him; and a hundred and twenty-seven dollars is just what Mr. Close paid Dan."

5

THE BLACK FOX SKIN

You must understand that from this time on, my association with November Joe was not continuous but fitful, and that after the events I have just written down I went back to Quebec, where I became once more immersed in my business. Of Joe I heard from time to time, generally by means of smudged letters obviously written from camp and usually smelling of wood smoke. It was such a letter, which, in the following year, caused me once more to seek November. It ran as follows:—

> Mr. Quaritch, sir, last week I was up to Widdeney Pond and I see a wonderful red deer buck. I guess he come out of the thick Maine woods to take the place o' that fella you shot there last fall. This great fella has had a accident to his horns or something for they come out of his head thick and stunted-like and all over little points. Them horns would look fine at the top of the stairs in your house to Quebec, so come and try for them. I'll be down to Mrs. Harding's Friday morning so as I can meet you if you can come. There's only three moose using round here, two cows, and a mean little fella of a bull.
> November.

This was the letter which caused me to seek Mrs. Harding's, but owing to a slight accident to the rig I was driven up in, I arrived late to find that November had gone up to a neighbouring farm on some business, leaving word that should I arrive I was to start for his shack and that he would catch me up on the way.

I walked forward during the greater part of the afternoon when, in trying a short cut through the woods, I lost my bearings and I was glad enough to hear Joe's hail behind me.

"Struck your trail 'way back," said he, "and followed it up as quick as I could."

"Have you been to Harding's?"

"No. I struck straight across from Simmons's. O' course I guessed it were probably you, but even if I hadn't known you was coming I'd a been certain you didn't know the country and was town-bred."

"How?"

"You paused wherever there were crossroads, and had a look at your compass."

"How do you know I did that?" I demanded again; for I had consulted my compass several times, though I could not see what had made Joe aware of the fact.

"You stood it on a log once at Smith's Clearing and again on that spruce stump at the Old Lumber Camp. And each time you shifted your direction."

I laughed. "Did you know anything else about me?" I asked.

"Knew you carried a gun, and was wonderful fresh from the city."

In answer to my laugh Joe continued:—

"Twice you went off the road after them two deer you saw, your tracks told me that. And you stepped in under that pine when that little drop o' rain fell. There wasn't enough of it to send a man who'd been a day in the woods into shelter. But I have always noticed how wonderful scared the city makes a man o' a drop o' clean rain-water."

"Anything else?"

"Used five matches to light your pipe. Struck 'em on a wore-out box. Heads come off, too. That don't happen when you have a new scraper to your box."

"I say, Joe, I shouldn't like to have you on my trail if I'd committed a crime."

Joe smiled a singularly pleasant smile. "I guess I'd catch you all right," said he.

It was long after dark when we reached November's shack that evening. As he opened the door he displaced something white which lay just inside it. He stooped.

"It's a letter," he said in surprise as he handed it to me. "What does it say, Mr. Quaritch?"

I read it aloud. It ran:—

> I am in trouble, Joe. Somebody is robbing my traps. When you get home, which I pray will be soon, come right over.
>
> S. Rone.

"The skunk!" cried November.

I had never seen him so moved. He had been away hunting for three days and returned to find this message.

"The darned skunk—" he repeated, "to rob *her* traps!"

"Her? A woman?"

"S. Rone stands for Sally Rone. You've sure heard of her?"

"No, who is she?"

"I'll tell you," said Joe. "Sal's a mighty brave girl—that is, she's a widow. She was married on Rone four years ago last Christmas, and the autumn after he got his back broke to the Red Star Lumber Camp. Didn't hump himself quick enough from under a falling tree. Anyway, he died all right, leaving Sally just enough dollars to carry her over the birth of her son. To make a long story short, there was lots of the boys ready to fill dead man Rone's place when they knew her money must be giving out, and the neighbours were wonderful interested to know which Sal would take. But it soon come out that Sal wasn't taking any of them, but had decided to try what she could do with the trapping herself."

"Herself?"

"Just that. Rone worked a line o' traps, and Sal was fixed to make her living and the boy's that way. Said a woman was liable to be as successful a trapper as a man. She's at it near three year now, and she's made good. Lives with her boy about four hours' walk nor'west of here, with not another house within five miles of her. She's got a young sister, Ruby, with her on account of the kid, as she has to be out such a lot."

"A lonely life for a woman."

"Yes," agreed November. "And now some skunk's robbing her and getting her frightened, curse him! How long ago was that paper written?"

I looked again at the letter. "There's no date."

"Nothing about who brought it?"

"No."

November rose, lighted a lantern, and without a word stepped out into the darkness. In five minutes he returned.

"She brought it herself," he announced. "Little feet—running—rustling to get home to the little chap. She was here afore Thursday morning's rain, some time Wednesday, not long after I started, I guess. . . . I'm off soon as ever I can stoke in some grub. You coming?"

"Yes."

Not much later I was following November's nimbly moving figure upon as hard a woods march as I ever care to try. I was not sorry when a thong of my moccasin gave way and Joe allowed me a minute to tie it up and to get my wind.

"There's Tom Carroll, Phil Gort, and Injin Sylvester," began November abruptly— "those three. They're Sally's nearest neighbours, them and Val Black. Val's a good man, but—"

"But what?" said I absently.

"Him and Tom Carroll's cut the top notches for Sally's favour so far."

"But what's that got to do with—"

"Come on," snapped November, and hurried forward.

I need say no more about the rest of the journey, it was like a dozen others I had made behind November. Deep in the night I could just make out that we were passing round the lower escarpments of a great wooded mountain, when we saw a light above glimmering through the trees. Soon we reached the lonely cabin in its clearing; the trees closed about it, and the night wind whined overhead through the bareness of the twigs.

Joe knocked at the door, calling at the same time: "It's me. Are you there, Sally?"

The door opened an inch or two. "Is it you, Joe?"

November thrust his right hand with its deep scar across the back through the aperture. "You should know that cut, Sal, you tended it."

"Come in! Come in!"

I followed Joe into the house, and turned to look at Sally. Already I had made a mental picture of her as a strapping young woman, well equipped to take her place in the race of life, but I saw a slim girl with gentle red-brown eyes that matched the red-brown of her rebellious hair, a small face, pale under its weather-tan, but showing a line of milk-white skin above her brows. She was in fact extremely pretty, with a kind of good looks I had not expected, and ten seconds later, I, too, had fallen under the spell of that charm which was all the more powerful because Sally herself was unconscious of it.

"You've been long in coming, Joe," she said with a sudden smile. "You were away, of course?"

"Aye, just got back 'fore we started for here. . . ." He looked round. "Where's young Dan?"

"I've just got him off to sleep on the bed there"; she pointed to a deerskin curtain in the corner.

"What? They been frightening him?"

Mrs. Rone looked oddly at November. "No, but if he heard us talking he might get scared, for the man who's been robbing me was in this room not six hours ago and Danny saw him."

November raised his eyebrows. "Huh! That's fierce!" he said. "Danny's rising three, ain't he? *He* could tell."

"Nothing at all. It was after dark and the man had his face muffled. Danny said he was a real good man, he gave him sugar from the cupboard!" said Sally.

"His hands . . . what like was his hands? . . . He gave the sugar."

"I thought of that, but Danny says he had mitts on."

November drew a chair to the table. "Tell us all from the first of it . . . robbing the traps and to-night."

In a few minutes we were drinking our tea while our hostess told us the story.

"It's more'n three weeks now since I found out the traps were being meddled with. It was done very cunning, but I have my own way of baiting them and the thief, though he's a clever woodsman and knows a heap, never dropped to that. Sometimes he'd set 'em and bait 'em like as if they were never touched at all, and other times he'd just make it appear as if the animal had got itself out. I wouldn't believe it at first, for I thought there was no one here-abouts would want to starve me and Danny, but it happened time after time."

"He must have left tracks," said Joe.

"Some, yes. But he mostly worked when snow was falling. He's cunning."

"Did any one ever see his tracks but you?"

"Sylvester did."

"How was that?" said Joe with sudden interest.

"I came on Sylvester one evening when I was trailing the rob-ber."

"Perhaps Sylvester himself was the robber."

Mrs. Rone shook her head.

"It wasn't him, Joe. He couldn't 'a' known I was comin' on him, and his tracks was quite different."

"Well, but to-night? You say the thief come here to-night? What did he do that for?' said Joe, pushing the tobacco firmly into his pipe-bowl.

"He had a good reason," replied Sally with bitterness. "Last Thursday when I was on my way back from putting my letter under your door, I come home around by a line of traps which I have on the far side of the mountain. It wasn't anything like my usual time to visit them, not but what I've varied my hours lately to try and catch the villain. I had gone about halfway to Low's Cor-ner—when I heard something rustling through the scrub ahead of me, it might have been a lynx or it might have been a dog, but when

I come to the trap I saw the thief had made off that minute, for he'd been trying to force open the trap, and when he heard me he wrenched hard, you bet, but he was bound to take care—not to be too rough."

"Good fur, you mean?"

"Good?" Sally's face flushed a soft crimson. "Good? Why I've never seen one to match it. It was a black fox, lying dead there, but still warm, for it had but just been killed. The pelt was fair in its prime, long and silky and glossy. You can guess, November, what that meant for Danny and me next winter, that I've been worrying about a lot. The whooping-cough's weakened him down bad, and I thought of the things I could get for him while I was skinning out the pelt." Sally's voice shook, and her eyes filled with tears. "Oh, Joe, it's hard—hard!"

November sat with his hands upon the table in front of him, and I saw his knuckles whiten as he gripped it.

"Let's hear the end of it!" he said shortly, man-like showing irritation when his heart was full of pity.

"The skin was worth eight hundred dollars anywhere, and I come home just singing. I fixed it at once, and, then being scared-like, I hid it in the cupboard over there behind those old magazines. I'd have locked it up, but I've nothing that locks. Who has on this section? Once or twice, being kind of proud of it, I looked at the skin, the last time was this morning before I went out. I *was* proud of it. No one but Ruby knew that I had got it. I left Ruby here, but Mrs. Scats had her seventh yesterday morning, and Ruby ran over to help for a while after she put Danny to bed. The thief must have been on the watch and seen her go, and he knew I was due to visit the north line o' traps and I'd be late anyway. He laid his plan good and clever. . . ."

She stopped for a moment to pour out another cup for Joe.

"Where's Ruby now?" he inquired.

"She's stopping the night; they sent over to tell me," replied Sally. "Well, to go on, I had a lynx in one of my traps which got dragged right down by Deerhorn Pond, so I was more than special late. Danny began at once to tell me about the man that came in. I rushed across and looked in the cupboard; the black fox pelt was gone, of course!"

"What did Danny say about the man?"

"Said he had on a big hat and a neckerchief. He didn't speak a word; gave Danny sugar, as I have said. He must 'a' been here some time, for he's ransacked the place high and low, and took near every pelt I got this season."

Joe looked up. "Those pelts marked?"

"Yes, my mark's on some—seven pricks of a needle."

"You've looked around the house to see if he left anything?"

"Sure!" Sally put her hand in her pocket.

"What?"

"Only this." She opened her hand and disclosed a rifle cartridge.

Joe examined it. "Soft-nosed bullet for one of them fancy English guns. Where did you find it?"

"On the floor by the table."

"Huh!" said Joe, and, picking up the lamp, he began carefully and methodically to examine every inch of the room.

"Any one but me been using tobacco in here lately?" he asked.

"Not that I know of," replied Sally.

He made no comment, but continued his search. At last he put down the lamp and resumed his chair, shaking a shred or two of something from his fingers.

"Well?" questioned Mrs. Rone.

"A cool hand," said November. "When he'd got the skin, he stopped to fill his pipe. It was then he dropped the cartridge; it came out of his pocket with the pipe, I expect. All that I can tell you about him is that he smokes 'Gold Nugget'"—he pointed to the shreds— "and carries a small-bore make of English rifle. . . . Hello! where's the old bitch?"

"Old Rizpah? I dunno, less she's gone along to Scats's place. Ruby'd take her if she could, she's that scairt of the woods; but Rizpah's never left Danny before."

Joe drained his cup. "We've not found much inside the house," said he. "As soon as the sun's up, we'll try our luck outside. Till then I guess we'd best put in a doze."

Mrs. Rone made up a shake-down of skins near the stove, and disappeared behind the deerskin curtain. Before sleep visited me I had time to pass in review the curious circumstances which the last few hours had disclosed. Here was a woman making a noble and plucky struggle to wring a living from Nature. In my fancy I saw her working and toiling early and late in the snow and gloom. And then over the horizon of her life appeared the dastardly thief who was always waiting, always watching to defeat her efforts.

When I woke next morning it was to see, with some astonishment, that a new personage had been drawn into our little drama of the woods. A dark-bearded man in the uniform of a game warden was sitting on the other side of the stove. He was a straightforward-looking chap getting on for middle age, but there was a certain doggedness in his aspect. Mrs. Rone, who was preparing breakfast, made haste to introduce him.

"This is Game Warden Evans, Mr. Quaritch," she said. "He was at Scats's last night. There he heard about me losing fur from the traps, and come right over to see if he couldn't help me."

Having exchanged the usual salutations, Evans remarked good-humouredly:—

"November's out trailing the robber. Him and me's been talking about the black fox pelt. Joe's wasting his time all right."

"How's that?" I asked, rather nettled, for wasting his time was about the last accusation I should ever have brought against my comrade.

"Because I can tell him who the thief is."

"You know!" I exclaimed.

Evans nodded. "I can find out any time."

"How?"

"Care to see?" He rose and went to the door.

I followed. It was a clear bright morning, and the snow that had fallen on the previous day was not yet melted. We stepped out into it, but had not left the threshold when Evans touched my shoulder.

"Guess Joe missed it," he said, pointing with his finger.

I turned in the direction indicated, and saw that upon one of the nails which had been driven into the door of the cabin, doubtless for the purpose of exposing skins to the warmth of the sun, some bright-coloured threads were hanging. Going nearer, I found them to be strands of pink and grey worsted, twisted together.

"What d'you think of that?" asked Evans, with a heavy wink.

Before I could answer, Joe came into sight round a clump of bush on the edge of the clearing.

"Well," called the game warden, "any luck?"

November walked up to us, and I waited for his answer with all the eagerness of a partisan. "Not just exactly," he said.

"What do you make of that?" asked Evans again, pointing at the fluttering worsted, with a glance of suppressed triumph at Joe.

"Huh!" said November. "What do you?"

"Pretty clear evidence that, ain't it? The robber caught his necker on those nails as he slipped out. We're getting closer. English rifle, 'Gold Nugget' in his pipe, and a pink and grey necker. Find a chap that owns all three. It can't be difficult. Wardens have eyes in their heads as well as you, November."

"Sure!" agreed Joe politely but with an abstracted look as he examined the door. "You say you found it here?"

"Yes."

"Huh!" said Joe again.

"Anything else on the trail?" asked Evans.

November looked at him. "He shot Rizpah."

"The old dog? I suppose she attacked him and he shot her."

"Yes, he shot her—first."

"First? What then?"

"He cut her nigh in pieces with his knife."

Without more words Joe turned back into the woods and we went after him. Hidden in a low, marshy spot, about half a mile from the house, we came upon the body of the dog. It was evident she had been shot—more than that, the carcass was hacked about in a horrible manner.

"What do you say now, Mr. Evans?" inquired Joe.

"What do I say? I say this. When we find the thief we'll likely find the marks of Rizpah's teeth on him. That's what made him mad with rage, and—" Evans waved his hand.

We returned to breakfast at Mrs. Rone's cabin. While we were eating, Evans casually brought out a scrap of the worsted he had detached from the nail outside.

"Seen any one with a necker like that, Mrs. Rone?" he asked.

The young woman glanced at the bit of wool, then bent over Danny as she fed him. When she raised her head I noticed that she looked very white.

"There's more'n one of that colour hereabouts likely," she replied, with another glance of studied indifference.

"It's not a common pattern of wool," said Evans. "Well, you're all witnesses where I got it. I'm off."

"Where are you going?" I asked.

"It's my business to find the man with the pink necker."

Evans nodded and swung off through the door.

November looked at Sally. "Who is he, Sally?"

Mrs. Rone's pretty forehead puckered into a frown. "Who?"

"Pink and grey necker," said Joe gently. A rush of tears filled her red-brown eyes.

"Val Black has one like that. I made it for him myself long ago."

"And he has a rifle of some English make," added November.

Mrs. Rone started. "So he has, but I never remembered that till this minute!" She looked back into Joe's grey eyes with indignation. "And he smokes 'Nugget' all right, too. I know it. All the same, it isn't Val!" The last words were more than an appeal; they were a statement of faith.

"It's queer them bits of worsted on the doornails," observed Joe judicially.

Her colour flamed for a moment. "Why queer? He's been here to see m—us more'n once this time back; the nails might, have caught his necker any day," she retorted.

"It's just possible," agreed November in an unconvinced voice.

"It can't be Val!" repeated Mrs. Rone steadily.

We walked away, leaving her standing in the doorway looking after us. When we were out of sight and of earshot I turned to November.

"The evidence against Black is pretty strong. What's your notion?"

"Can't say yet. I think we'd best join Evans; he'll be trailing the thief."

We made straight through the woods towards the spot where the dog's body lay. As we walked I tried again to find out Joe's opinion.

"But the motive? Haven't Mrs. Rone and Black always been on good terms?" I persisted.

Joe allowed that was so, and added: "Val wanted to marry her years ago, afore Joe Rone came to these parts at all, but Rone was a mighty taking kind of chap, laughing and that, and she married him."

"But surely Black wouldn't rob her, especially now that he has his chance again."

"Think not?" said Joe. "I wonder!" After a pause he went on. "But it ain't hard to see what'll be Evans's views on that. He'll say Val's scared of her growing too independent, for she's made good so far with her traps, and so he just naturally took a hand to frighten her into marriage. His case ag'in' Val won't break down for want of motive."

"One question more, Joe. Do you really think Val Black is the guilty man?"

November Joe looked up with his quick, sudden smile. "It'll be a shock to Evans if he ain't," said he.

Very soon we struck the robber's trail, and saw from a second line of tracks that Evans was ahead of us following it.

"Here the thief goes," said Joe. "See, he's covered his moccasins with deerskin, and here we have Evans's tracks. He's hurrying, Evans is—he's feeling good and sure of the man he's after!"

Twice November pointed out faint signs that meant nothing to me.

"Here's where the robber stopped to light his pipe—see, there's the mark of the butt of his gun between those roots—the snow's thin there. Must 'a' had a match, that chap," he said after a minute, and standing with his back to the wind, he made a slight movement of his hand.

"What are you doing?" I asked.

"Saving myself trouble," he turned at right angles and began searching through the trees. "Here it is. Hung up in a snag. . . . Seadog match he used." Then, catching my eye, he went on: "Unless he was a fool, he'd light his match with his face to the wind, wouldn't he? And most right-handed men 'ud throw the match thereabouts where I hunted for it."

Well on in the afternoon the trail led out to the banks of a wide and shallow stream, into the waters of which they disappeared. Here we overtook Evans. He was standing by the ashes of a fire almost on the bank.

He looked up as we appeared. "That you, Joe? Chap's took to the water," said the game warden, "but he'll have to do more than that to shake me off."

"Chap made this too?" inquired November with a glance at the dead fire.

Evans nodded. "Walked steady till he came here. Dunno what he lit the fire for. Carried grub, I s'pose."

"No, to cook that partridge," said Joe.

I glanced at Evans, his face darkened, clearly this did not please him.

"Oh, he shot a partridge?"

"No," said Joe; "he noosed it back in the spruces there. The track of the wire noose is plain, and there was some feathers. But look here, Evans, he didn't wear no pink necker."

Evans's annoyance passed off suddenly. "That's funny!" said he, "for he left more than a feather and the scrape of a wire." The game warden pulled out a pocketbook and showed us wedged between its pages another strand of the pink and grey wool. "I found it where he passed through those dead spruces. How's that?"

I looked at Joe. To my surprise he threw back his head, and gave one of his rare laughs.

"Well," cried Evans, "are you still sure that he didn't wear a pink necker?"

"Surer than ever," said Joe, and began to poke in the ashes.

Evans eyed him for a moment, transferred his glance to me, and winked. Before long he left us, his last words being that he would have his hands on "Pink Necker" by night. Joe sat in silence for some ten minutes after he had gone, then he rose and began to lead away southeast.

"Evans'll hear Val Black's the owner of the pink necker at Lavette Village. It's an otter's to a muskrat's pelt that then he'll head straight for Val's. We've got to be there afore him."

We were. This was the first time I had experience of Joe's activities on behalf of a woman, and, to begin with, I guessed that he himself had a tender feeling for Sally Rone. So he had, but it was not the kind of feeling I had surmised. It was not love, but just an instinct of downright chivalry, such as one sometimes finds deep-set in the natures of the men of the woods. Some day later I may tell you what November was like when he fell head over ears in love, but that time is not yet.

The afternoon was yet young when we arrived at Val Black's. At that period he was living in a deserted hut which had once been used by a bygone generation of lumbermen.

It so happened that Val Black was not at home, but Joe entered the hut and searched it thoroughly. I asked him what he was seeking.

"Those skins of Sally's."

"Then you do think Black . . ."

"I think nothing yet. And here's the man himself anyway."

He turned to the door as Val Black came swinging up the trail. He was of middle height, strongly built, with quick eyes and dark hair which, though cropped close, still betrayed its tendency to curl. He greeted November warmly; November was, I thought, even more slow-spoken than usual.

"Val," he said, after some talk, "have you still got that pinky necker Sally knitted for you?"

"Why d' you ask that?"

"Because I want to be put wise, Val."

"Yes, I've got her."

"Where?"

"Right here," and Black pulled the muffler out of his pocket.

"Huh!" said Joe.

There was a silence, rather a strained silence, between the two. Then November continued. "Where was you last night?"

Val looked narrowly at Joe, Joe returned his stare.

"Got any reason fer asking?"

"Sure."

"Got any *reason* why I should tell you?"

"Yes to that."

"Say, November Joe, are you searching for trouble?" asked Black in an ominously quiet voice.

"Seems as if trouble was searching for me," replied November.

There was another silence, then Val jerked out, "I call your hand."

"I show it," said Joe. "You're suspected of robbing Sally's traps this month back. And you're suspected of entering Sally's house last evening and stealing pelts . . ."

Val fell back against the doorpost.

"Stealin' pelts. . . . Sally's?" he repeated. "Is that all I'm suspected of?"

"That's all."

"Then look out!" With a shout of rage he made at Joe.

November stood quite still under the grip of the other's furious hands.

"You act innocent; don't you, you old coyote!" he grinned ironically. "I never said *I* suspected you."

Black drew off, looking a little foolish, but he flared up again.

"Who is it suspects me?"

"Just Evans. And he's got good evidence. Where was you between six and seven last night?"

"In the woods. I come back and slep' here."

"Was you alone?"

"Yes."

"Then you can't prove no alibi." Joe paused.

It was at this moment that Evans, accompanied by two other forest rangers, appeared upon the scene. He had not followed the track, but had come through a patch of standing wood to the north of the hut. Quick as lightning he covered Black with his shotgun.

"Up with your hands," he cried, "or I'll put this load of bird-shot into your face."

Black scowled, but his hands went up. The man was so mad with rage that, I think, had Evans carried a rifle he would not have submitted, but the thought of the blinding charge in Evans's gun cowed him. He stood panting. At a sign, one of the rangers sidled up, and the click of handcuffs followed.

"What am I charged with?" cried Black.

"Robbery."

"You'll pay me for this, Simon Evans!"

"It won't be for a while—not till they let you out again," retorted the warden easily. "Take him off up the trail, Bill."

The rangers walked away with their prisoner, and Evans turned to Joe.

"Guess I have the laugh of you, November," he said.

"Looks that way. Where you takin' him?"

"To Lavette. I've sent word to Mrs. Rone to come there to-morrow. And now," continued Evans, "I'm going to search Black's shack."

"What for?"

"The stolen pelts."

"Got a warrant?"

"I'm a warden—don't need one."

"You'll not search without it," said November, moving in front of the door.

"Who'll stop me?" Evans's chin shot out doggedly.

"I might," said Joe in his most gentle manner.

Evans glared at him. "You?"

"I'm in the right, for it's ag'in' the law, and you know it, Mr. Evans."

Evans hesitated. "What's your game?" he asked.

Joe made a slight gesture of disclaimer.

Evans turned on his heel.

"Have it your way, but I'll be back with my warrant before sun up to-morrow, and I'm warden, and maybe you'll find it's better to have me for a friend than—"

"Huh! Say, Mr. Quaritch, have you a fill of that light baccy o' yours? I want soothin'."

As soon as Evans was out of sight, Joe beckoned me to a thick piece of scrub not far from the hut.

"Stay right here till I come back. Everything depends on that," he whispered.

I lay down at my ease in a sheltered spot, and then Joe also took the road for Lavette.

During the hours through which I waited for his return I must acknowledge I was at my wits' end to understand the situation. Everything appeared to be against Black, the cartridge which fitted his rifle, the strands of the telltale neckerchief, the man's own furious behaviour, his manifest passion for Mrs. Rone, and the suggested motive for the thefts—all these things pointed, conclusively it seemed to me, in one direction. And yet I knew that almost from the beginning of the inquiry November had decided that Black was innocent. Frankly, I could make neither head nor tail of it.

The evening turned raw, and the thin snow was softening, and though I was weary of my watch I was still dreaming when I started under a hand that touched my shoulder. Joe was crouching at my side. He warned me to caution, but I could not refrain from a question as to where he had been.

"Down to the store at Lavette," he whispered. "I was talking about that search-warrant—pretty high-handed I said it was, and the boys agreed to that."

Then commenced a second vigil. The sun went down behind the tree roots, and was succeeded by the little cold wind that often blows at that hour. Yet we lay in our ambush as the dusk closed quickly about us, nor did we move until a slight young moon was sending level rays between clouds that were piling swiftly in the sky.

After a while Joe touched me to wakefulness, and I saw something moving on the trail below us. A second or two of moonlight gave me a glimpse of the approaching figure of a man, a humped figure that moved swiftly. If ever I saw craft and caution inform an advance, I saw it then.

The clouds swept over, and when next the glint of light came, the dark figure stood before the hut. A whistle, no answer, and its hand went to the latch. I heard Joe sigh as he covered the man with his rifle. Then came his voice in its quiet tones.

"Guess the game's off, Sylvester. Don't turn! Hands up!"

The man stood still as we came behind him. At a word he faced round. I saw the high cheekbones and gleaming eyes of an Indian, his savage face was contracted with animosity.

"Now, Mr. Quaritch," said November suggestively.

I flatter myself I made a neat job of tying up our prisoner.

"Thank you. What's in that bundle on his back?"

I opened it. Several skins dropped out. Joe examined them. "All got Sally's mark on," he said. "Say, Mr. Quaritch, let me introduce you to a pretty mean thief."

I noticed that Joe took our prisoner along at a good pace towards Lavette. After a mile or two, however, he asked me to go ahead, and if I met with Mrs. Rone to make her wait his arrival, but he added, in an aside, "Tell her nothing about Sylvester."

I reached the village soon after dawn, but already the people were gathered at the store, where every one was discussing the case. Evans sat complacently listening to the opinions of the neighbours. It was clear to me that the public verdict was dead against Black. Some critics gave the rein to venomous comments which made me realize that, good fellow as Val was, his hot temper had had its effect on his popularity.

As I heard nothing of Mrs. Rone, I set out towards her house. When I met her I noticed that her gentle face wore a changed expression. I delivered my message.

"I'll never speak to November again as long as I live!" she said with deep vindictiveness.

I feebly attempted remonstrance. She cut me short.

"That's enough. November's played double with me. I'll show him!"

I walked beside her in silence and, just before we came in sight of the houses, we met with Joe alone. He had evidently left Sylvester in safe custody. Joe glanced from Sally to me. I read understanding in his eyes.

"We've got him trapped safe, Sally. Not a hole for him to slip out by."

Sally's rage broke from her control. "You're just too cute, November Joe," she blazed, "with your tracking and finding out things, and putting Val in jail! What do you say to it that I've been fooling you all the time? I never lost no pelts! I only said it to get the laugh against ye. Ye was beginning to believe ye could hear the muskrats sneezing!"

"Is that so?" inquired Joe gently.

"Yes, and I'm going into Lavette this minute to tell them!"

Joe stepped in front of her. "Just as you like, Sally. But how'll ye explain these?" He flung open the bundle of skins he carried.

Mrs. Rone turned colour. "Where did ye find them?" she gasped.

"On his back!"

She hesitated a moment, then, "I gave Val that lot," she said carelessly.

"That's queer, now," said Joe, "'cos it was on Injin Sylvester I found them."

Sally stared at Joe, then laughed suddenly, excitedly. "Oh, Joe! you're sure the cutest man ever made in this world!" And with that she flung her arms round his neck and kissed him.

"I'd best pass that on to Val Black!" said Joe calmly.

And Sally's blushes were prettier than you could believe.

There is no need for me to tell how Black was liberated from the hands of the crestfallen Evans, who was as nonplussed as I myself had been at the breakdown of the case, which up to the last moment had on the face of it seemed indestructible.

I have never looked forward to any explanation, more than that which November gave to Mrs. Rone, Black, and myself the same evening.

"It was the carcass of Rizpah give me the first start," said Joe. "As soon as I saw that I knew it weren't Val."

"Why?" asked Sally.

"You remember it was hacked up? Now here was the case up to that. A thief had robbed Sally and all the sign he left behind was a few threads of his necker and an English-made cartridge. The thief goes out and old Rizpah attacks him. He shoots her. Then he cuts her body nigh to pieces. Why?" We all shook our heads.

"Because he wants to get his bullet out of her. And why does he want to get his bullet? Only one possible reason. Because it's different to the bullet he dropped *on purpose* in the house."

"By Jove!" I cried.

"From that it all fits in. It seems funny that the thief should drop a cartridge, funnier still that he shouldn't notice he'd left a bit of his necker stuck to the nails on the door. Still, I'd allow them two things might happen. But when it came to his having more bits of his necker torn off by the spruces where Evans found them, it looked like as if the thief was a mighty poor woodsman. *Which he wasn't.* He hid his tracks good and cunning. After that I guessed I was on the right scent, but I wasn't plumb sure till I come up to the place where he killed the partridge. While he was snaring it he rested his rifle ag'in' a tree. I saw the mark of the butt on the ground, and the scratch from the foresight upon the bark. Then I knew he didn't carry no English rifle."

"How did you know?" asked Sally.

"I could measure its length ag'in' the tree. It was nigh a foot shorter than an English rifle."

Val's fist came down on the table. "Bully for you, Joe!"

"Well, now, there was one more thing. Besides that black fox Sally here missed other marked pelts. They wasn't much value. Why did the thief take them? Again, only one reason. He wanted 'em for making more false evidence ag'in' Val."

He paused. "Go on, Joe," cried Mrs. Rone impatiently.

"When Mr. Quaritch and I came to Val's shack we searched it. Nothing there. Why? 'Cos Val had been home all night and Sylvester couldn't get in without wakin' him."

"But," said I, "wasn't there a good case against Black without that?"

"Yes, there was a case, but his conviction wasn't an absolute cinch. On the other hand, if the stolen skins was found hid in his shack . . . That's why you had to lie in that brush so long, Mr. Quaritch, while I went in to Lavette and spread it around that the shack hadn't been searched by Evans. Sylvester was at the store and he fell into the trap right enough. We waited for him and we got him."

"O' course," continued Joe, "revenge on Val weren't Sylvester's only game. He meant robbin' Sally, too, and had his plan laid. He must 'a' first gone to Val's and stole a cartridge and the bits of necker before he robbed Sally's house. Last night he started out to leave a few cheap pelts at Val's, but he had the black fox skin separate in his pack with a bit o' tea and flour and tobacco, so if we hadn't took him, he'd have lit out into Maine an' sold the black fox pelt there."

"But, Joe," said Sally, "when I came on Sylvester that evening I told you of when I was trailing the robber, how was it that his tracks and the robber's was quite different?"

"Had Sylvester a pack on his back?"

"Yes. Now I think of it, he had."

"Then I dare bet that if you'd been able to look in that pack you'd 'a' found a second pair o' moccasins in it. Sylvester'd just took them off, I expect. It was snowing, weren't it?"

"Yes."

"And he held you in talk?"

"He did."

"Till the snow covered his tracks?"

"It's wonderful clear, Joe," said Mrs. Rone. "But why should Sylvester have such a down on Val?"

Joe laughed. "Ask Val!"

"Ten years ago," said Val, "when we was both rising twenty year, I gave Sylvester a thrashing he'd likely remember. He had a dog what weren't no use and he decided to shoot it. So he did, but he didn't kill it. He shot it far back and left it in the woods . . . and I come along . . ."

"The brute!" exclaimed Sally.

"He's a dangerous Injin," said November, "and he's of a breed that never forgets."

"When he gets out of prison, you'll have to keep awake, Joe," said Val.

"When he gets out, I'll have the snow in my hair all right, and you and Sally'll be old married folks," retorted Joe. "You'll sure be tired of each other by then."

Sally looked at Val and Joe caught the look.

"Leastways," he added, "you'll pretend you are better'n you do now."

We all laughed.

6

THE MURDER AT THE DUCK CLUB

November Joe had come to Quebec to lay in his stores against the winter's trapping. He had told me that the best grounds in Maine were becoming poorer and poorer and that he had decided to go in on the south side of the St. Lawrence, somewhere beyond Rimouski.

I knew that November was coming since two hours before his arrival a cable had been brought in for him, for when in Quebec, although he stayed at a downtown boardinghouse, he was in the habit of using my office as a permanent address. I was therefore not at all surprised to hear his soft voice rallying my old clerk in the outer office. A more crabbed person than Hugh Witherspoon it would be impossible to meet, but it cannot be denied that like so many others he had a kindliness for November. Presently there was a knock at the door and Joe, his hat held between his two hands, sidled into the room. He was never quite at ease except in the open, and as he came towards me with his shy smile, his moccasins fell noiselessly on the polished boards.

I handed him his telegram, which he opened at once. It ran:—

> Offer you fifty dollars a day to come at once to Tamarind Duck Club.
> Eileen M. East.

Joe whistled and characteristically said nothing.

"Who is Eileen M. East?" I asked.

Joe made no reply for a moment, then he indicated the telegram and said:—

"This has been redirected from Lavette. Postmaster Tom knew I'd be in to see you. Miss East was one of an American party I was with, 'way up on Thompson's salmon river this spring."

At this moment a clerk knocked and entered, bringing with him a second telegram. Joe read it:—

> You must come. Murder done. A matter of life
> and death. Please reply.
>   Eileen M. East.

"Will you write out an answer for me?" asked Joe.

I nodded. Joe is slow with the pen.

"'Miss Eileen M. East.' Please put that, sir, and then 'arriving on 3.38,' and sign."

"How shall I sign it?" said I.

"Just write 'November.'"

I did so, and ringing again for the clerk I directed him to give the telegram to the boy who was waiting. There was a moment's silence, then—

"Can you come along, Mr. Quaritch?"

I looked at the business which had accumulated on my desk, for, as I have had occasion to observe more than once, I am a very busy man, indeed, or, at least, I ought to be, for my interests, as were those of my father and grandfather, are bound up with the development of the Dominion of Canada and range through the vegetable and mineral kingdoms to water-power and the lighting of many of our greatest cities.

"Yes, but I must have ten minutes in which to give Witherspoon his instructions."

Joe went to the door. "The boss wants you right away, old man," I heard him say.

Witherspoon shuffled into my room.

"I'll go and get a rig," continued November, "and have it waiting outside. We haven't overmuch time if we're going to call at your country place for your outfit."

A quarter of an hour later Joe and I were bowling along in the rig drawn by a particularly good horse. I live with my sister some distance out on the St. Louis road, and thither we drove at all speed.

My sister had gone out to tea with some friends, but she is well accustomed to my always erratic movements, so that I felt quite at ease when I left a note explaining that I was leaving Quebec for a day or two with November Joe.

We reached the station just in time and were soon steaming along through the farmlands that surround Quebec City.

You who read this may or may not have heard of the Tamarind Duck Club. It is a small association composed chiefly of Montreal and New York business men, to which I had leased the sporting rights of a chain of lakes lying on one of my properties not very far from the waters of the St. Lawrence. To these lakes the ducks fly in from the tide each evening, and in the fall very fine sport is to be obtained there, the guns often averaging ten and twenty brace of birds, the latter number being the limit permitted to each shooter by the rules. During the season there are generally two or three members at the clubhouse, which, though but a log hut, is warm and comfortable. In fact, the Tamarind Club has a waiting list of those who desire to belong to it quite out of all proportion to its capacity.

All these facts marshalled themselves and passed through my mind as the train rolled on, and at length I said to Joe:—

"Murder done at the Tamarind Club! It seems incredible. It must be that some poacher has shot one of the guides."

"Maybe," said Joe, "but Miss East said 'a matter of life and death'; what can that mean? That's what I'm asking myself. But here we are! It won't be long before we know a bit more."

The cars drew up at the little siding which is situated within a walk of the Tamarind Club. We jumped down just as a girl, possessing dark and vivid good looks of a quite arresting kind, stepped from the agent's office and caught November impulsively by the hand.

"Oh, Joe, I *am* so glad to see you!"

November Joe always had a distinct appeal to women; high and low, whatever their station in life, they liked him. Of course, his looks were in his favour. Women generally do find a kind glance for six foot of strength and sinew, especially when surmounted by a perfectly poised head and features such as Joe's. He had a curious deprecating manner, too, that carried its own charm, and he appeared unable to speak two sentences to any woman without giving her the impression that he was entirely at her service—which, indeed, he was.

"When I got your message from Lavette, I come right along," said the woodsman simply; "Mr. Quaritch come, too. It's from him the club holds its lease."

Miss East sent me a flash of her dark eyes, and I saw they were full of trouble.

"I hope you will be on my side, Mr. Quaritch," she said. "Just now I need friends badly."

"What is it, Miss Eileen?" asked Joe, as she paused.

"Uncle has been shot, Joe."

"Mr. Harrison?"

"Yes."

"I'm terrible sorry to hear that. He was a fine, just man."

"But that is not all. There is something even worse! . . . They say it was Mr. Galt who shot him."

"Mr. Galt!" exclaimed November in surprise. "It ain't possible!"

"I know! I know! Yet every one believes that he did it. I sent for you to prove to them that he is innocent. You will, won't you, Joe?"

"I'll sure do my best."

I saw her struggle for self-control; the way she got herself in hand was splendid.

"I must tell you how it happened," she said, "and we can be walking on at the same time, for I want you, Joe, to see the place before dark. . . . Yesterday afternoon there were five of us at the club. I was the only woman and the men settled to go out after the ducks in the evening, for though it had been wet all day, the wind went round and it began to blow clear about three o'clock. Four shooters went out; there was uncle and Mr. Hinx, and Egbert Simonson, and—and Ted Galt."

"Is that the same Mr. Hinx who was salmon-fishing with us early this year?"

"Yes. . . . Most evenings I go with uncle, but yesterday the bush was so wet that I decided not to go, so the four men went, and at the usual time the others all came back. At half-past seven, I began to get anxious, so I sent Tim Carter, the head guide, to see if anything was wrong. He found my uncle dead in his screen."

"And what brought Mr. Galt's name into it?"

She hesitated for a second.

"He and uncle had a good way to go to their places, which were next each other. They walked together, and their voices were heard, very loud, as if they were quarrelling. Egbert Simonson complained about it when he came in . . . said they made enough noise to disturb the lake, and after that, of course, Ted was suspected."

"Did Mr. Galt own they'd had any words?" inquired Joe.

"Yes. Uncle was angry with him," she admitted, and a colour showed for a moment in her cheeks. "Ted is not a rich man, Joe; you know that."

"Huh!" said Joe with complete comprehension. Then, after a pause, he asked: "Who is it suspects Mr. Galt?"

"It was Tim Carter who got the evidence together against him."

"*Evidence?*"

"Uncle and Ted were placed next each other at the shoot."

"And had Mr. Harrison or Mr. Galt the outside place?"

"Ted had."

"Well, who was on the other side of your uncle? I suppose there must have been someone."

"It was Mr. Hinx."

"Then what makes Carter so sure it was Mr. Galt done it?"

"Ah! That is the awful thing. My uncle was killed with number six shot."

"Yes?"

"And Ted is the only one who uses number six size. The others all had number four."

Joe whistled, and was silent for some moments. Then he said:—

"I think, Miss Eileen, I'd as soon you didn't tell me any more. I'd like best to have Mr. Galt's and Carter's stories at first-hand from theirselves."

The girl stopped short. "But, November, you don't believe it was Ted!"

"I sure don't," he said. "Mr. Galt ain't that kind of a man. Where is he?"

"Didn't I tell you? Some police came out on the last train. They have him under arrest. It is dreadful!"

Half an hour later November Joe was face to face with Carter, who gave him no very warm welcome, and added nothing to the following statement, which he had dictated to the police inspector and signed in affidavit form:—

"Last evening roundabout five o'clock, four members of the club, Harrison, Hinx, Simonson, and Galt, started out for Reedy Neck. Reedy Neck is near half a mile long by a hundred yards wide. It is a kind of a promontory of low ground that sticks out into Goose Lake. The members walked to their places. I did not accompany them, because I had been ordered to take a canoe round to the north side of the lake, so as I could move any ducks that might pitch on that part of the lake over the guns. There are six screens on Reedy Neck. Before starting, the members drew lots for places as per Rule 16. Galt drew number one, that is the screen nearest the end of the Neck and farthest from the clubhouse. Harrison got number two. Number three was unoccupied. Hinx was in number four, and Simonson in number five.

"Reedy Neck is covered along its whole length with bush and rushes, and the gunners cannot see one another. The screens consist of sunk pits with facings of rushes and alders.

"The shooting began before I was round to the north side, and continued till it was dark. Several hundred ducks flew in from the estuary. I waited about ten minutes after the last shot was fired and then went back to the clubhouse. When I got there, I found Harrison had not returned. I heard this from Simonson, who was angry because, he said, Harrison and Galt had talked in loud, excited tones as they went to their places.

"He was annoyed because he was of opinion that their voices had frightened some bunches of duck at which he might have got a shot.

"At half-past seven Miss East, niece to Harrison, came into the clubhouse kitchen, where I was at the time arranging to have the dead ducks picked up. You cannot pick them up while the flight is on because of scaring the others. When the wind is from the north, like it was last evening, it drifts the dead birds on to the south shore of Goose Lake. I told Noel Charles and Vinez, two of the club under-guides, to see about the pick-up. Miss East told me that her Uncle Harrison had not come in, and I had better go and see what was keeping him. She was afraid that he might have got bogged in the swamp, as it was dark. She was worried-like, and Sitawanga Sally, the Indian squaw cook, tried to cheer her. She said the path from Reedy Neck was easy to follow.

"I left Miss East with Sally and went out. There was a bit of moonlight. I went down to Reedy Neck and found Harrison in number two screen. He was dead, and already stiff. I concluded he must have shot himself by accident. I lifted the body to carry it back. When I was about fifty yards from the club I shouted. Galt came running out. I told him Harrison had shot himself. He said, 'Good God! How awful for Eilie!'

"Miss East had heard me, and was with us the next minute. She was greatly put about.

"We carried the body in and laid it on a bed. It was then I looked at the wound for the first time. Sally, the cook, was with me to lay out the body.

"I said: 'He couldn't have shot himself this way.'

"I said this because I saw the shot had spread so much that I knew it could not have been fired at very close quarters. Sally agreed with me. I do not know whether her opinion is worth anything. It may be. Most Indian women of sixty years old have seen dead men. I put my finger in the wound and drew out a shot. We then covered up the body with a point-four blanket and left it.

"I locked the door and took away the key. I did this because the wound was a dreadful one, and I thought it better that Miss East should not see the body. I then went to the gun-room and compared the shot I had taken from the wound with other sizes. It was a number six shot. The only club member who uses number six shot is Mr. Galt. Harrison, Simonson, and Hinx all use number four. I said nothing to any one about the number six shot.

"At dawn I went back to Reedy Neck and worked out all the details. It was easy, for they were plain in the soft mud. There was no sign of any one except Galt having passed number two screen. His returning footsteps were along the edge of the water until he came to number two screen where Harrison was. Then his tracks led up the silt towards it. He must have been within twelve paces of Harrison. There he paused, as I could tell by the tracks. I suggest it was then that he fired the shot. Next he went back to the edge of the lake and continued towards the clubhouse.

"After making this examination I spoke to Simonson, the senior member. I understand that he cabled for the police.

"Signed, T. Carter."

I read out this statement while November listened with the curiously minute attention that he always accorded to the written or printed word. When I had finished he forbore to ask any questions, but expressed a desire to speak with Galt. We found him in the custody of a tall young trooper, who, at the command of the inspector, considerately left us to ourselves.

Joe shook hands gravely and warmly.

"Now, Mr. Galt, I'm right sorry about all this, and glad that Miss Eileen sent for me."

"She sent for you?" cried Galt.

"Sure."

"That's the best news I've had since I was arrested. It shows that she believes I am innocent."

"'Course she does!" said Joe. "And now will you tell me everything you can remember of what happened yesterday, before Mr. Harrison was found dead?"

Galt was silent for a moment.

"Here goes!" he said at length. "I'll begin at the beginning. In the early afternoon I went for a walk in the woods with El—Miss East. I asked her to marry me. She said yes. I'm not a rich man, though I'm not exactly a poor one."

"No," agreed Joe, to whom a tenth of Galt's income would have been riches beyond his farthest dream.

"Anyway," continued Galt, "we guessed we might have trouble with her uncle, Mr. Harrison, and, on the principle of not shirking a bad talk, we arranged that I was to take the first opportunity of putting Mr. Harrison wise as to the position of affairs. By the time we returned to the clubhouse, we found Hinx, Simonson, Harrison, and Guide Carter just starting for the evening flight. I joined them, and, as luck would have it, I drew the next screen to Mr. Harrison. Simonson and Hinx went off together, and I was left with Harrison, so I started in and told him how Eileen and I had fixed to get married."

Joe gave the sideways jerk of the head which signified his comprehension.

"He was furious," went on Galt, "even more angry than I expected a judge—he was a judge in the States—would ever be. He accused me of being after her dollars rather than herself."

"He couldn't 'a' really thought that," said Joe judicially; "that is, unless he was blind."

Galt smiled.

"Thanks, November, Eilie always told me you were a courtier of the woods. As to Harrison, I dare say he would not have been so hard on me, only unfortunately I had crossed him once or twice in matters about the club. I blackballed a fellow he proposed this spring."

"Blackballed? What does that amount to?" inquired Joe.

"Opposed his becoming a member."

"That so? Go on."

"As I was telling you, he gave me the rough side of his tongue. I begged him not to decide in a hurry, as we meant to get married anyway, but we'd sooner do it with his good will. That, of course, made him madder than ever. So, seeing I was not likely to do any good just then, I left him and went to my own screen, which was next to his at the very end of the Neck."

"Where did you leave him?"

"About fifty yards on this side of his screen."

"And after that?"

"I had not been ten minutes in my screen when the ducks began to come in. They kept on coming. I must have fired between seventy and eighty cartridges. Harrison, too, was banging away."

"Could you see him?"

"No, the reeds are too high, but more than once I saw the ducks he shot fall. I could see them because they were twenty or thirty yards high in the air."

Joe nodded.

"At a quarter past six the flight was pretty well over and the firing along the line grew less and less frequent. At the half-past it had stopped altogether, and I decided to go back to the clubhouse."

"One minute," put in Joe. "What time was it when Harrison fired the last shot that you remember?"

"It must have been about ten minutes past six."

"Did any birds pass over him after that?"

"I thought so."

"And he did not fire at them?"

"No."

"Were you not surprised at that?"

"Not very. It was pretty dark, and Harrison was not a quick shot."

"Now tell me all the details you can call to mind of your walk back to the club."

"I picked up my gun and my cartridge bags, which were nearly empty, and walked along the edge of the water until I was opposite Harrison's screen. There I paused. I thought I'd have another try to persuade him. I called out his name. There was no answer. So I walked up the mudbank and shouted again."

"From the top of the bank? Could you see into the screen?"

"Partially, but it was dark, and as I did not catch sight of Harrison I concluded he had already returned to the club, so I retraced my steps to the edge of the water and came back to the club myself."

"You met no one on the way?"

"I fancied I saw a figure on the south shore."

"Whereabouts?"

"About opposite number three screen on Reedy Neck."

"Have you nothing more to tell me?"

"No, I can't remember anything more. But I want to ask you this question. Why have I been arrested? There can be but little evidence against me."

November looked Galt in the face. "I wish that was so," he said, "but it ain't. You see, Mr. Harrison was killed with number six shot."

"What of that?"

"You are the only club member who uses that size."

"Good Heavens!"

"See here, Mr. Galt," went on Joe, "there's that fact of the shot, and there's the fact that your tracks are the only ones that pass Mr. Harrison's screen; besides which the quarrel between you was overheard."

"It is a chain of coincidences—a complete chain," cried Galt in dismay.

Joe nodded and left the room without more words.

As soon as we were clear of the building I asked him what he thought of it all.

He turned the question on me. "And what do you think?"

"The evidence against Galt is about as strong as it need be," I said sorrowfully. "Here we have a man shot in a screen. The only person who passed anywhere near was the prisoner. The deed was done with number six shot; the only man using number six is again the prisoner. When you add to that the quarrel, which was a pretty hot one by all accounts, why, you have as complete a case as any prosecution need wish to handle."

"That's so," agreed Joe. "And the worst of it is that Galt's own story don't help us any."

"Do you believe he is telling the truth?"

"That's the one thing that I do believe."

I demurred.

"Well, you know, if he had been telling lies," said Joe, "he'd have made a better story of it, wouldn't he? Let's get along to Reedy Neck."

So to Reedy Neck we went. For the benefit of my readers I must describe it. Reedy Neck is a promontory of mud and rush which extends, as I have said, some eight hundred yards into the lake. At no point does it rise twelve feet above the level of the water.

From the moment that he set foot upon it, November Joe examined every yard of ground with infinite care, and as he walked kept up a running commentary upon the tracks and their, to him, obvious story. At first there were many footprints, but presently these thinned to two.

"Look here," said Joe. "The tapped boots is Harrison and the moccasins is Galt. Here must have been the spot where Galt told Harrison he was going to marry Miss Eileen. See, Harrison stopped, stamped back on his heels, and drove down the butt of his gun into the mud."

"Yes, I see."

"And here," continued Joe, "they separated. Harrison's tracks go up the bank, Galt's passes on. We'll follow Galt's first."

Which we did. They led us straight to the duck screen he had occupied. Crouching in it as he would have done, we found that a sea of reeds shut in the view on every side. The mud floor of the screen was covered with empty shells.

"That's where he knelt waiting for the ducks," said Joe, pointing to a circular cavity; "his knee made that. There's little to be learnt here."

And we began to follow Galt's trail back. The returning tracks ran along a lower line by the edge of the water, until nearly opposite the scene of the tragedy they swerved at right angles, and went up the bank to within a few yards of the screen where Harrison's body had been found.

"He stopped here," said Joe, "stopped for quite a while. Now, Mr. Quaritch, I'll see what I can find out."

"You'll not find much," said a voice behind us. "At least, not much that has not been found out before. If I was you, November, I'd give it up as a bad job. Galt done it. The tracks is plain as print."

"There's some says that print don't always tell the truth, Tim Carter," answered Joe sturdily.

Carter, a powerful, stubborn-faced woodsman, with wild brown hair and small side-whiskers, began to walk forward, but Joe held up his hand.

"Stand you back, Tim," said he, "I don't want you rooting around and tearing up the ground with your feet."

Carter sat down beside me on a driftwood log that lay among the reeds, and together we watched November; I with sympathy, for Miss East's eager hopes lived in my consciousness. Carter's face, however, wore an expression of supercilious amusement.

Such a methodical examination I had rarely seen Joe make, and that very fact damped my expectations. First of all he followed out every line of tracks. Then he made a series of measurements, and last of all began to pick up and look over the gun wads which lay about in great numbers. Suddenly he darted forward, and picked up one that lay close beside my foot.

"You are both witnesses where I found this," he cried.

Carter rose. "I'll mark the place if you like," he said with a laugh.

"That's good! Do it."

Carter thrust a stick into the ground. "Now," asked he, "what next?"

But Joe was paying no attention. He was engaged in examining the piece of driftwood from which we had risen, and the shore near the water in its vicinity. At length, evidently satisfied, he came to me.

"I want you to take charge of this," he said, handing me the gun wad; "it'll likely be needed in evidence."

Carter listened and grinned. "Finished, Joe?"

"Yes, here."

"Whereaway next?"

"To the south shore."

"Want me along?"

"Please yourself."

It was a long walk, undertaken in silence. The two woodsmen were obviously antagonistic. Carter, being pleased to believe Galt guilty, was consequently full of suspicion towards any attitude of mind that seemed to question his conclusions. November's point of view I had not fathomed. It is possible that he could see light where to me all was utter darkness. On the other hand, I could not, as I have said, conceive a more convincing chain of evidence than that which had led Carter straight from the crime to Galt—the quarrel, the number six shot, the fact that Galt had been within ten yards of the murdered man's hiding-place about the time the murder must have been committed.

I went all over it again. There seemed no break, and when I thought of Eileen East, I groaned in spirit. She believed in Galt, and, even more for her sake than for his, I longed for November to confound the sullen Carter, though how this much-to-be-desired end might be brought about I failed to see.

At length we reached the south shore.

"Any one been round this side to-day?" asked Joe.

"Can't say. If they have, you're such a plumb-sure trail-reader, you'll know, won't you?" Carter retorted grimly.

Without answering, Joe signed to us to remain where we were, while he crossed and cut diagonally from the lake shore to the mountain. After that he went down to the boathouse where the canoes were kept. A moment later his voice rose in a call. We found him looking into one of the canoes.

"When was this one last out?" he asked.

"Not since Friday."

"That's funny," said Joe.

We followed his pointing finger. In the bottom of the boat was a little pool of blood.

"Can you account for that, Tim Carter?"

"Vinez and Noel Charles must have taken the canoe when they picked up the shot ducks this morning," said Carter.

"They didn't go near the boathouse," returned Joe. "I found their tracks. They lead down by the hill over there."

"I suppose you think this blood's got something to do with the murder?" sneered Carter.

"I'm sure inclined that way," said Joe.

As we walked back to the clubhouse my mind was in a whirl. I have already said that I could see little daylight through the tangle of signs and clues, and now I was aware that the prospect looked more complicated than ever. As we approached the clubhouse, Miss East, who had evidently been watching for us, ran out.

"Well," she cried breathlessly, "what have you done? Have you found out everything?"

"I'll want to look over the members' guns before I answer that," said Joe.

"They are all in the gun-room."

We entered a little annex to the club where the guns were kept. Carter picked out one. "Here's Galt's."

Joe lifted it carelessly. "Twelve calibre," said he, examining it.

"Sure," said Carter. "All the others uses twelves, except Simonson. His is number ten."

"Which of them has two guns?"

"Only Simonson."

"Where are they?"

"Here's the one he used last night."

"And the fellow to it... his second gun?"

"In the case there."

Joe picked out the weapon, fitted it together, and looked it over attentively. Then with equal care he took it apart and replaced it in the case.

"Joe, have you nothing to tell me? Joe!" cried Miss East, her face vivid with fear and hope.

"I'd like to ask Sitawanga Sally a question," said November, "and maybe Mr. Galt might as well hear it."

At a sign from Eileen, Carter, with a look of deep disgust on his face, went to fetch the woman and the suspected man. Galt came in first, accompanied by the police inspector. Meanwhile Joe had taken up Galt's gun and glanced through the barrels. As Sitawanga Sally entered, he snapped it to.

She was a full-blooded Indian and, like many of her race, now that the first bloom of youth was past, she might have been any age. Her high cheekbones and wispy hair surrounded sullen eyes. She stood and fixed them on Joe with an expressionless stare. November returned it.

"Say, Sally," said he, at last. "What for you kill old man Harrison?"

"No, no! Me not kill 'um! Galt kill 'um!" she replied, showing her yellow fangs under a bulging upper lip.

Joe shook his head. "It don't go any, Sally," said he. "I know you shot him with Mr. Simonson's second gun in the case over there."

"Me no kill 'um! Me no kill 'um!" she cried.

Her arms, raised high for a moment in excitement, dropped suddenly, and she fell again into the stoicism which was her normal condition.

"You'd better put in your facts, Joe," said the inspector briskly.

"I'm free to own," began November in his soft, easy manner, "that it was quite a while before I could see anything to shake Carter's evidence. My mind was made up it wasn't Galt done it, so it must 'a' been somebody else. . . . But I could find no tracks—only Galt's and Carter's, and Carter's bore out his story right enough. Consequently I set out to look for a third person, and it was plain that the only way a third person could have come was in a canoe.

"Yet there wasn't no signs of a canoe being beached, though I searched careful for them. Still I knew the shot was never fired from the water, which was too far off from where Mr. Harrison's body was found for that to be possible. So you see it only left me one way out. Some one come in a canoe, stepped out on the big driftwood log lying near the screen, walked up along it to the end, and shot Mr. Harrison from there.

"Now the distance from the log to Mr. Harrison's body is about eleven yards, and yet the shot had not spread much—we saw that—so I guessed, whoever he was, the murderer must've used a chokebore gun that threw the shot very close and strong, and I began to think the thing must have been done with a bigger bore gun than a twelve. So I started to search afresh, and in time I found a wad (Mr. Quaritch there has it)—a ten-bore wad recently fired.

"Now, Mr. Harrison had a twelve-bore and so'd Mr. Galt. The only man who owned a ten was Mr. Simonson, and he was the farthest away of all in the screen near the clubhouse. Besides, he was wearing boots with nails in the soles, and he could never 'a' walked down that bit of driftwood without leaving pretty clear traces. So it weren't him, but I got pretty certain it were some one using a full-choke ten-bore and wearing either moccasins or rubbers. Another point, the murder weren't done on impulse, but whoever was guilty had thought it all out beforehand."

"Why do you say that?" chipped in the officer.

"The number six shot. There weren't no ten-bore shells loaded with number six. The one who done it must have loaded them cartridges o' purpose to bring suspicion on Mr. Galt."

"I see."

"Well," went on Joe. "That's as far as the examining of Reedy Neck took me, and there was nothing better left to do but to go round and have a look at the canoes. Besides, Mr. Galt told me and Mr. Quaritch he'd seen some one moving about there on the south shore just after the time the murder was committed. So round we went, and there, sure enough, I come on the tracks of a pair of small moccasins leading down to the canoe house and coming up again.

"'Sitawanga Sally,' says I to myself, 'those footmarks looks mighty like yours.'"

"But the blood, the blood in the canoe—it couldn't have been Harrison's?"

"No, it weren't," said Joe. "It were Sally's own. She's weak and them ten-bore guns kicks amazing. I guessed it bled her nose. Look at her swelled cheek and lip."

All the time, as Joe's words proved how he had drawn the net round her, I watched the stoic face of the Indian squaw. When he pointed to her swollen mouth, her features took life, and an expression of the wildest and most vindictive passion that I have ever seen flashed out upon them. Recognizing the hopelessness of her position she threw aside all subterfuge.

"Yes, me kill 'um Harrison!" she cried. "Me kill 'um good!"

"Oh, Sally," cried Eileen. "He was always so kind to you!"

"Harrison devil!" answered the Indian woman passionately. "Me swear kill 'um Moon-of-Leaves time. Harrison kill 'um Prairie Chicken—my son."

"What does she mean?" Eileen looked round wildly at us.

"I think I can tell you that," said the inspector. "Moon-of-Leaves means June, and wasn't Mr. Harrison a judge back in the States?"

"Yes."

"And he had sometimes to deal with the Indians from the Reserve. I remember hearing this woman's son got into trouble for stealing horses."

"Bad man say Prairie Chicken steal 'um," broke in Sally. "Black clothes—black clothes—men talk-talk. Then old man Harrison talk. Take away Prairie Chicken—far, far. Me follow."

"That's so," said the inspector. "I remember some judge tried Prairie Chicken, and gave him ten years. It may hev been Judge Harrison. The Chicken died in gaol. If that is so, it explains everything. Indians never forget."

"Prairie Chicken, he dead. Me swear kill 'um Harrison. Now Prairie Chicken happy. Me ready join 'um," said the old squaw, and relapsed once more into her stolid silence.

"She thought Mr. Harrison was directly responsible for the death of her son," added the inspector.

"Poor woman!" said Eileen.

There is not much to add. Subsequent inquiries confirmed the inspector's facts and made it clear that Sitawanga Sally, learning that Harrison belonged to the Tamarind Club, had taken service there for the direct purpose of avenging her son. No doubt she noticed the affection which was growing up between Eileen and Galt, and attempted to incriminate the latter so as to obtain a fuller measure of revenge as well as to draw suspicion away from herself.

Blood for blood is still the Indian creed. It is simple and it is direct.

I think the whole case was best summed up by November himself:—

"I guess our civilized justice does seem wonderful topsy-turvy to them Indians sometimes," said he.

7

THE CASE OF MISS VIRGINIA PLANX

November Joe and I had been following a moose since day-break, moving without speech. We had not caught even a glimpse of the animal; all that I had seen were the huge, ungainly tracks sunk deep in swampy ground or dug into the hillsides.

Suddenly from somewhere ahead there broke out the sound of two shots, and, after a minute, of two more.

"That's mean luck," said November. "It'll scare our moose, sure. Pity! He's got a fine set o' horns, more'n fifty-six inches in the spread."

"How can you tell that? You haven't seen him?"

Joe's grey eyes took on the look I now knew well.

"I'm certain sure they spread not less than fifty-six and not more'n sixty. . . . My! Look out! Them shots has put him back. He's coming to us!"

There was a crashing in the undergrowth sounding ever nearer, and soon a magnificent bull-moose came charging into sight.

"He's your moose!" said Joe, as my shot rang out. "You hit him fair behind the shoulder. No need to shoot again."

The great brute, weighing over twelve hundred pounds, was stumbling forward in his death-rush; all at once he collapsed, and silence reigned once again in the forest. We ran up. He was quite dead. I turned to Joe.

"Now we'll be able to measure his horns," I said, a little maliciously; for, to tell the truth, I thought Joe had been drawing me when he pretended to be able to tell within four inches the measurements of the antlers of a moose which he had not seen.

"Let's have that fine steel measuring-tape you carry," said Joe.

I produced it, and he stretched it across the horns.

"Fifty-eight inches," said he.

I looked at my hunter.

"It ain't nothing but simple," he said. "I see the scrape of his horns over and over ag'in where he passed between the spruces. You can always tell the size of horns that way."

I laughed. "Confound you, Joe! You always—"

But here I was checked. *Bang, bang!* went the rifle in the distance, and again, *Bang, bang!* After an interval the shots were repeated.

"Two shots going on at steady intervals," said Joe. "That's a call for help. There they go again. We'd best follow them up."

We travelled for half an hour, guided by the sounds; then Joe stopped.

"Here's his trail—a heavy man not used to the woods."

"I can see he's heavy by the deep prints," said I. "But why do you say he's not used to woods? He's wearing moccasins, isn't he?"

"Sure he is." November Joe pointed to the tracks. "But he's walking on his heels and on the sides of his feet. A man don't do that unless his feet is bruised and sore."

We hurried on, and soon came in sight of a man standing among the trees. We saw him raise his rifle and fire twice straight upwards to the sky.

"It's Planx!" said Joe in surprise.

"What? The millionaire you went into the woods with to locate timber last year?"

"The identical man."

As we approached, Joe hailed him. Planx started, and then began to move as quickly as he could towards us. He was a thick-shouldered, stout man, his big body set back upon his hips, his big chin thrust forward in a way that accentuated the arrogance of his bulging lips and eyes.

"Can you guide me to the house of November— Ho! It's you, Joe!"

"Yes, Mr. Planx."

"That is lucky, for I need your help. I need it as no man has ever needed it before."

"Huh! How's that?"

"My daughter was murdered yesterday."

The words made me gasp, and not me only.

"Miss Virginny!" cried Joe. "You can't mean that. Nobody would be brute enough to kill Miss Virginny!"

Planx made no reply, but stared at Joe in a sombre and convincing silence.

"When did it happen?"

"Some time before five o'clock yesterday evening. But I'll put you wise as we walk. I'm stopping at Wilshere's camp, four miles along. Ed told me you lived round here, and I set out to find you."

As we walked Planx gave us the following facts: It appeared that he had been spending the last two weeks in a log hut which had been lent him by a friend, Mr. Wilshere. His household consisted of one servant,—his daughter's nurse, a middle-aged woman whom they had brought with them from New York,—two guides, and a man cook. On the previous day Miss Virginia had taken her rod after lunch, as she had often done before, and gone off to the river to fish.

"What hour was it when she left?" asked November.

"Half-past one. About three o'clock one of the guides who was cutting wood near the river saw her. She had put down her rod and was reading a book. At five I went to join her. She was not there. Her rod lay broken and there were signs of a struggle and the tracks of two men. I shouted for Ed, the old guide. He came running down and we took up the trail. It led us straight over to Mooseshank Lake. The ruffians had put her in our own canoe and gone out on the lake."

Planx paused, and presently continued:—

"We went round the lake and found on the far side the spot where they had beached the canoe. Leading up into the woods from that point, we again struck the trail of the two men, but my daughter was no longer with them."

"Are you sure of that?"

"As certain as you'll be yourself later on. From the river to the lake the tracks showed they were carrying her. When they left the canoe they were going light. They must have drowned her in the lake. It's clear enough. Presently I saw something floating on the water, it was her hat."

"Had Miss Virginny any jewelry on her?" asked Joe.

"A watch and a necklace."

"What value?"

"Seven or eight hundred dollars."

"Huh," said November reflectively. "And what did you do after finding her hat?"

"We trailed the two villains until they got on to some rocky ground. It was too dark then to do more, so we returned. Ed (he's the best tracker of my two guides) got away at dawn to see if he couldn't puzzle out the trail."

"Did he?"

"He had not returned when I started for your place."

"We've only three hours daylight left," said Joe. "Let's travel."

Which we did, the huge Planx, for all his unwieldy build, keeping up wonderfully well.

In about an hour we reached the river. A man was standing on the bank.

"Any luck, Ed?" shouted Planx.

"Couldn't find another sign among them rocks."

Planx turned to Joe. "Five thousand dollars if you lay hands on them," he said. "You, Ed, go back to the house and see if there's any news."

Joe was already at work. By the river the traces were so plain that any one could read them—the slender feet of the victim and the larger footprints of the two men. The fishing-rod, snapped off towards the top of the middle joint, had been left where it had fallen. It seemed as if the girl had tried to defend herself with it.

When he examined this spot, Joe made one or two casts up and down the bank, hovering here and there while Planx stood on the top of the slope and gloomily watched him. Now and then he asked a question.

"She started fishing about an acre downstream, got her line hung up twice, and the second time lost her fly. She had a fish on after that, but never landed it," said Joe in reply.

"Bah! How do you know all this?" growled Planx.

"First time her tracks show where she disengaged her hook from a tree; next time I see the hook sticking in a branch. As to the fish, it's plain enough. First she runs upstream, then down, then up again, then back in a bit of a circle—must have been a heavy fish that made her move about like that. Now let's get to the lake."

November literally nosed his way along. The moccasined tracks of the two men showed faintly here and there on the softer parts of the ground.

"Looks as if they was toting something," said Joe. "They must 'a' carried her. Stop! They set her down here for a spell."

Another moment brought us over the rise and in sight of Mooseshank Lake. I halted involuntarily.

The lake lay black and still upon the knees of a great mountain. Forests climbed to the margin and looked down into its depths on the one side; on the other the water lapsed in slow pulsations on a beach of stones, that stretched beneath bare and towering cliffs. Sunshine yet blazed upon the treetops, but the lake was already sunk in shadow. The place seemed created for the scene of a tragedy.

November had pushed on to the spot where footprints and other signs showed where the men had entered the canoe. The deep slide of a moccasined foot in the mud seemed to tell of the effort it required to get the girl embarked.

"They took her out on the lake and murdered her!" groaned Planx. "Dragging? There's no use dragging, that water goes plumb down to the root of the world. It was surveyed last year by Wilshere's people, and they could get no soundings."

After that we went round to the other side of the lake, and saw the beached canoe. The two sets of moccasined tracks showed clearly on the strip of mud by the water, but were soon lost in the tumbled debris of a two-year-old stony landslip over which trailing appeared quite impossible. November was busy about this landing-place for a longer time than I expected, then he crossed the landslide at right angles and disappeared from our view.

"There's a stream over there comes in a little waterfall from the cliffs," said Planx, pointing after Joe. "You can hear it."

That was all the conversation that passed between us until Joe returned. He came hurrying towards us.

"Say, Mr. Planx," he began.

"What is it?"

"She isn't dead."

"What?"

"Anyways, she wasn't when she passed here."

"Then where are her tracks?" demanded Planx, pointing to the footprints on the mud. "Those were made by two full-sized men."

"Aye," said Joe, "maybe I can tell you more about that later. But I have a proof here that you will think mighty good." He drew out a little leather case I had given him, and extracted from it a long hair of a beautiful red-gold colour. "Look at that! I found it in the spruces above there."

Planx took it gently in his great fingers. He was visibly much moved. For a few seconds he held it without speaking, then, "That grew on Virginia's head sure enough, Joe. Is it possible my girl is alive?"

"She is, sure! Don't be afeared, you'll soon have news of her. I can promise you that, Mr. Planx. This wasn't no case of murder. It's just an abduction. They'd never be such fools as to kill her! They're cuter than that. Isn't she your daughter? They'll hold her to big ransom. That's their game."

An ugly look came into Planx's eyes. "That's their game, is it? I'm not a man that it is easy to milk dollars from," said he.

By this time it was growing too dark for Joe to work any longer. We crossed the lake with Planx, and that night Joe and I camped near the end of Mooseshank Lake, where a stream flowed from it.

"We're not far from the little waterfall and the string of water that drops from it down the hill near the landslip," said Joe. "I want to get back there early in the morning, and this is the nearest way."

But after events altered his intentions.

At dawn, while we were having breakfast, Joe stood up and stared into the trees that grew thick behind us. As he called out, I looked back and saw the indistinct figure of a man in their shadow watching us. He beckoned, and we approached him. I saw he was young, with a pale face and rather shabby town-made clothes.

"Don't you remember Walter Calvey, November?" he said, holding out his hand. "I was with you and Mr. Planx, and—and—her last year in the woods."

"Huh, yes, and what are you doing here, Mr. Calvey?" asked Joe, shaking hands.

"I heard about Virginia—how could I keep away after that?" exclaimed Calvey.

"You've no cause to fret yet," said Joe.

"What? When they've killed her! I'll go with you, and if we can find those—"

"Huh! She's not dead! Take my word for it!" Joe's grey eyes gave me a roguish look. "Why, I've got a thing here in my pocketbook you'd give me a hundred dollars for!" He held the red-gold hair up to the light of the rising sun.

Calvey shook from head to foot.

"Virginia's! You couldn't find its match in Canada! Tell me—"

"I can't wait to tell you and you can't wait to hear. Light out now. Old man Planx could make it unhealthy for you."

"You're right! He hates me because Virginia won't marry Schelperg, of the Combine. He hasn't let us meet for months. And more than that, he's ruined me and my partner in business. It was easy for a rich man to do that," added Calvey bitterly.

"You go and start into business again," advised Joe. "I'll send you word first thing I know for certain."

But it was some time before he could induce Calvey to leave us. After he had gone, I wondered whether Joe suspected him of having a hand in spiriting away Virginia. Presently I asked him.

Joe shook his head. "He couldn't have done it if he wanted to! He's a good young chap, but look at his boots and his clothes—he was bred on a pavement, but he's Miss Virginny's choice for all that. We'll start now, Mr. Quaritch, just where I found that bit of gold caught in a branch that hangs over the little stream up above there. You see, she lost her hat, and she has a splendid lot of hair, and so when I could find no tracks,—for they came down the bed of the stream,—I searched 'bout as high as her head. I guessed she'd be liable to catch her hair in a branch."

But we had hardly started when we heard the voice of Planx roaring in the wood below us. He was coming along at an extraordinary pace in spite of his ungainly, rolling stride.

"You were right, Joe, Virginia is alive! It is a case of abduction. See what I have here."

He held a long stick or wand in his hand. The top of the wand was roughly split, and a scrap of paper stuck in the cleft.

"Ed's just found this in the canoe on the lake," he went on. "These blackguards must have come back in the night and put it there."

"What have they said in the paper?" asked November.

"*You must pay to get your daughter back. If you want our terms, come to the old log camp on Black Lake to-morrow night. No tricks. We have you rounded up, sure. Don't try to track us, or we will make it bad for her.*'"

Joe took the stick and examined it with care.

"They meant to leave it stuck in the ground Indian fashion," said I, for I had seen letters of Indians made conspicuous in this way by lonely banks of rivers and other places where wandering hunters pass.

"They meant to do that, but found the canoe handy." Joe touched the ends of the wand. "Green spruce wood, cut near their camp," said he.

"There's plenty of spruce like that right here," objected Planx; "why do you say it was cut near their camp?"

"It's cut and split with a heavy axe, such as no man ever carries about with him. Well, we'd best do no more tracking till we see the chaps that has Miss Virginny. It's Black Lake tonight, then?"

"Yes, meet me by the alder swamp that's west of Wilshere's place," said Planx.

He stayed talking for a while, and after he was gone we shifted our camp to a more convenient spot and waited for the evening.

Black Lake lies at a distance of some five miles from Wilshere's, and as it abounded in grey trout, a log hut had been built for the convenience of the occasional fishermen who visited it. Starting early we came in sight of the lake while the glow was still in the western sky.

On the way, Planx made known to us his plan of campaign. It was a simple one. He would get the men into the hut, and speak them fair till a favourable moment presented itself, when he would demand the surrender of his daughter under threat of shooting the kidnappers if they refused or demurred.

"There are three of us, and we can fix them easy," said Planx.

November Joe shook his head. "They're not near such big fools as you think them," he remarked.

We had stopped on some high ground in the shelter of the woods, from which we could see the fishing-hut. Planx took a look round with his field glass.

"No sign of life anywhere," he said.

In fact, when we approached it after darkness had fallen, the place seemed entirely deserted. Nevertheless, Joe signed to us to wait while he went on to reconnoitre. He vanished with his silent, Indian-like glide, his movements as inaudible as those of a ghost. In about five minutes a light suddenly sprang up in the hut and Joe's voice called us.

As we entered the door, I saw Joe had kindled a lantern and was pointing to a piece of paper which lay on the rough-hewn table.

Planx seized upon it.

"The same writing as before. Listen to this: '*If you will swear to give us safe conduct, we will come to talk it out. If you agree to this, wave the lantern three times on the lake shore, and that will mean you give your oath to let us come and go freely.*'"

"I told you they were not fools," said Joe. "What's the orders now, Mr. Planx?"

Planx handed Joe the lantern. "Go and wave the lantern."

From the door of the hut we watched November as he walked down to the lake. At the third swing of the light, a voice hailed him.

"You hear? They were waiting in a canoe," said Planx to me. "That's cute."

Then followed the splash of paddles and the rasp of the frosted rushes as the canoe took the shore. Joe had returned by this time, and hung up the lantern so that it lit the whole of the hut. Then the three of us stood together at one side of the table.

Our visitors hesitated outside the door.

"There are only two of them," whispered Planx.

As he spoke, a short, bearded man, in a thick overcoat, stepped into the light, followed by a tall and strongly built companion. Both wore black visor masks, with fringe covering the mouth. I noticed they were shod in moccasins.

"Evenin'," said the tall man, who was throughout the spokesman.

To this no one made any reply, so, after a second or so, he went on.

"My partner and me is come to make you an offer, Mr. Planx. We've got your daughter where you'll never find her, where you'd never dream of looking for her."

"Don't be too sure of that," growled Planx.

The tall man passed over the remark without notice.

"If we agree on a bargain, she shall be returned to you unhurt three days from the time the price is paid over. And that price is one hundred thousand dollars.

"Those are our terms. The question for you is, do you want your daughter, or do you not?"

The next incident was as swift as it was unexpected.

"I conjecture that is something of an easy question to answer," said Planx in his slow tones. "In fact I—"

On the word he slipped out a revolver. But quick as was Planx's hand to carry out the impulse of his brain, Joe's was quicker. He knocked the revolver from Planx's grasp.

"You treacherous dog, Planx!" cried the kidnapper. "Is that how you keep faith? Well, we have a reply to that, too. We offered to give up the girl for one hundred thousand dollars, now we make the price one hundred and fifty thousand!"

"I'll never pay a cent of it!" shouted Planx.

"When you come to change your mind," replied the kidnapper quietly, "just hang a white handkerchief on one of the trees at the edge of this wood. Then put the money in notes in that tin on the shelf. Leave us two clear days, and you'll get your girl back safe. But if you monkey, it will be the worse for her."

Without more words, the two masked men left the hut, and before long we heard the sound of their paddles upon the water. For a few moments we listened until the noise died away, then, like the explosion of a thunderstorm, Planx opened upon Joe.

November faced the storm with an entirely placid aspect until I began to wonder at his patience. But when at last he spoke, the other fell dumb as if Joe had struck him.

"That's settled, Mr. Planx. You've done with me, and I've done with you. Now quiet down and out!"

Planx opened his lips as if to speak, but, seeing Joe's face, he changed his mind and rushed from us into the darkness.

At once Joe put out the light. "We can't trust Planx just at the moment. He's fair mad. But we'll have him back in half an hour to show him the way back to Wilshere's," he remarked with a chuckle.

And in fact this was exactly what happened. It was a subdued but still a very resentful Planx whom we escorted through the dark woods. On our way back to our camp Joe made a detour to examine the tracks of the kidnappers by the light of the lantern which he had carried with him.

As had been the case by Mooseshank Lake, so now we found the trails very clear near the waterside. Joe studied them for a long time.

"What do you make of them?" asked he, at last.

"Moccasins—there are the footprints of one of the same men as we saw before, I think," I answered.

Joe nodded.

"Well, you're out of it now at any rate," said I.

"And what about my promise to Calvey?" he rejoined. "I'm deeper in it than ever. I've got to find Miss Virginny sure."

"You can't track her because of that threat in the letter to Planx?"

"That's so, and I have another reason ag'in' it."

"What is it?"

"That I'll be speaking to Miss Virginny herself before to-morrow night," said Joe quietly, nor, having made this dramatic announcement, would he say more.

The next morning Joe was early astir.

"What are you going to do to-day?" said I.

"I'm going to find out the name of the man that has Miss Virginny hid away. If you'll wait here, Mr. Quaritch, I'll come back as soon as I've done it. You've got your rod and there's plenty of fish in the lake."

With that I had to be content. Through the pleasant morning hours I fished, but my mind was not on the sport. Instead, I was puzzling over the facts of the disappearance of Miss Virginia Planx. Before starting, Joe had laid a bet with me that he would come back with the name of her abductor, and I was wondering what clue he had to go upon. Hardly any that I could think of—the trail of the two men and the golden hair, very little more. Yet November had committed himself in the matter, and he was not a man to talk until he could make good his words. I must own the hours passed very slowly while the sun reached and then began to decline from the zenith.

About two o'clock, I heard November hail me.

"What about the bet?" I called on sight of him. "Who pays?"

"You pay, Mr. Quaritch," said Joe.

"Why, who is it, then?"

"A fellow called Hank Harper."

"Why, I've heard of him. He passes for a man of high character."

Joe laughed. "All the same, he's the chap who done it," said he. "I expect he's got her up at his cabin on Otter Brook."

"Look here, November," I said. "You tell me Hank Harper is in the kidnapping business, and I believe you, because I've never known you speak without solid facts behind you; but I think you owe me the whole yarn."

Joe pulled out his pipe. "All right, Mr. Quaritch. We've some time to put in, anyway, before we need start to go to Harper's, and I'll spend the time in showing you how I lit on Hank. To begin at the beginning. There are two of them. One's this man Harper. I don't know who the other is, and it don't much matter. If we find Harper, we find his partner. Well, Miss Virginny was fishing when they stole down upon her and carried her off. I've already told you what happened until they took to the canoe. They paddled across the lake and the two men got out, leaving Miss Virginny in the canoe to paddle herself round and land elsewhere."

"But surely she could have escaped," I cried.

"She was under their rifles, and had to do exactly what she was ordered. I found where she'd landed, and followed her tracks to that little waterfall stream, and it was there I found the golden hair. So far, you see, everything fitted in together as good as the jaws of a trap, and the message on the bit of paper about a ransom carried it further on. So did the talk we had with Harper—it must have been him did the speaking—at Black Lake. When I knocked up Planx's revolver, I was wonderful sorry to have to do it, but a promise is a promise, and he'd passed his word for a safe-conduct. After, when my eyes fell upon the trail left by Harper's partner, I knew I never done a better act in my life."

"Explain, Joe!"

"That trail showed me I'd been wrong in my notions of the business, wrong from beginning to end."

"Wrong? Why, as you said yourself, it fits in all along."

"Did you take any notice of that trail?" inquired Joe.

"It seemed an ordinary trail, with nothing special about it."

"Wasn't there? It give me a start, I can tell you, Mr. Quaritch! You see all the weight was in the middle of the moccasin. The heels and toes were hardly marked at all."

November looked at me as if expecting me to see the meaning of this peculiarity, but I shook my head.

"It meant that the foot inside the moccasin was a very little one, a good bit shorter than the moccasin."

"You can't mean—" I began.

"Yes," said Joe. "The second person at Black Lake wasn't a man at all, but just Miss Virginny herself!"

"Well, if that was so, why she had the game in her hands then,— she had only to appeal to us,—to speak."

Joe interrupted me. "Hers was another sort of game. You see I'm pretty sure that Miss Virginny has kidnapped herself, or at any rate consented to be kidnapped!" He waited for this amazing statement to sink in before he continued. "The minute I come to that fact, I knew that my notion about her being covered with their rifles at the lake and all that was wrong, plumb wrong. She had just paddled round and joined the two men later; and then, when I come to think over it careful, I saw how I might raise the name of the man that was helping her."

"It does not look an easy thing to do," I said.

Joe smiled. "I lit out for Wilshere's camp, and asked the woman if there was anything of Miss Virginny's missing from her room. She said there wasn't. Then I saw my way a bit. I was in the woods with Miss Virginny last year, and I know she's mighty particular about personal things. I don't believe she could live a day without a sponge and a comb, and most of all without a toothbrush—none of them high-toned gals can. Isn't that so?"

"Yes, that is so, but—"

"Well," went on November, "if she went of her own free will, as I was thinking she did—or else why did she come to Black Lake?— if, as I say, I was right in my notion, and she'd made out the plans and kidnapped herself, the man who was with her would be only just her servant, in a manner of speaking. And I was certain that one of the first things she'd do would be to send him to some store to buy the things she wanted most. She couldn't get her own from Planx's camp without giving herself away, so she was bound to send Hank to hike out new ones from somewhere."

"What happened then?"

"I started in on the stores roundabout this country, and with luck I stepped into the big store at Lavette, and asked if any one had been buying truck of that kind. They told me Hank Harper. I asked just what. They said a hairbrush, a comb, a couple of tooth-brushes, and some other gear. That was enough for me. They weren't for Mrs. Hank, who's a half-breed woman, and don't always remember to clean herself o' Saturdays."

"I see," said I.

"The things was bought yesterday, so it all fits in, and there's no more left to find out but why Miss Virginny acted the way she has, and that we'll know before to-morrow."

It was well on towards ten o'clock that night before we reached Harper's cabin on Otter Brook. At first we knocked and knocked in vain, but at length a gruff voice demanded angrily what we wanted.

"Tell Miss Virginny Planx that November Joe would like a word or two with her."

"Are you drunk," shouted the man, "or only crazy?"

"I've tracked her down fair and square and I've got to see her."

"I tell you she isn't here."

"Let me in to make sure for myself."

"If a man comes to my door with a threat, I'll meet him with my rifle in my hand. So you're warned," came from the cabin.

"All right, then I'll start back to report to Mr. Planx."

On the words the door opened and a vivid, appealing face looked out. "Come in, dear Joe," said a honeyed voice.

"Thank you, Miss Virginny, I will," said Joe.

We entered. A lamp and the fire lit up the interior of a poor trapper's cabin, and lit up also the tall slim form of Miss Virginny Planx. She wore a buck-skin hunting shirt belted in to her waist, and her glorious hair hung down her back in a thick and heavy plait. She held out her hand to Joe with one of the sweetest smiles I have ever seen or dreamed of.

"You're not going to give me away, dear Joe, are you?" said she.

"You've given yourself away, haven't you, Miss Virginny?"

Virginia Planx looked him in the eyes, then she laughed. "I see that I haven't. But can I speak before this gentleman?"

Joe hastened to vouch for my discretion, while Hank Harper nursed his rifle and glowered from the background, where also one could discern the dark face of the half-breed squaw. But Miss Virginia showed her complete command of the situation.

"Coffee for these two, please, Mrs. Harper," she cried, and while we were drinking it she told us her story.

"You-maybe heard of old Mr. Schelperg, of the Combine?" she began. "My father wanted to force me to marry him. Why he's fifty by the look of him, and . . . I'd much rather drown myself than marry him."

"There's younger and better-looking boys around, I surmise, Miss Virginny?" returned November meaningly.

Virginia flushed a lovely red. "Why, Joe, it's no use blinding you, for you remember Walter Calvey, don't you?"

"Sure! So it's him. That's good. But I heard he was out of his business," said Joe with apparent simplicity.

"I must tell you all, or you won't understand what I did or why I did it. My father ruined Walter, because that would anyhow put off our marriage. Then, when the Schelperg affair came on and he gave me no rest, I could not stand it any longer. You see, he is so clever he would pay all my bills, no matter how heavy, but he never let me have more than five dollars in my pocket, so that I was helpless. I could never see Walter, nor could I hear from him, and all the time Schelperg was given the run of the house."

November was audibly sympathetic, and so was I.

"Then one day this notion came to me, I planned it all out, and got Hank to help. (I'd have asked you, dear Joe, if you'd been there.) Come now, Joe, you must see how good a pupil I was to you, and how much I remembered of your tracking, which I used to bother you to teach me."

"You're right smart at it, Miss Virginny!"

"I arranged the broken rod, and Hank and his brother carried me to the canoe, then they got out on the other side of the lake and

I paddled up near to the rock by the waterfall, to put the police or whoever should be sent after me off my trail. I'm real hurt I didn't deceive you, Joe."

"But you did right through—till you come to Black Lake," Joe assured her.

"But you did not recognize me then?" she cried, "and I'd put on a pair of Hank's moccasins to make big tracks!"

November explained, and added the story of his dismissal by Planx.

"Well, it's lucky you were there, anyhow, or we'd have had poor Hank shot. That fixed me in my determination to get the money. I want it for Walter, I want to make up to him for all that my father has made him lose."

"So Mr. Calvey is in this, too?" said Joe in a queer voice.

"If you mean that he knows anything about it, you're absolutely wrong!" exclaimed Virginia passionately. "If he knew, do you think he'd ever take the money? It's going to be sent to him without any name or clue as to where it comes from. Walter is as straight a man as yourself, November Joe!" she added proudly. "You know him and yet you suspected him!"

"I didn't say I did. I was asking for information," said Joe submissively. "But you haven't got the money yet."

"No! But I'll get it in time."

And in the end Miss Virginia triumphed. She received her ransom in full, and it is to be doubted if Mr. Planx ever had an idea of the trick played on him. And I'm inclined to think Mr. Walter Calvey is still in the dark, too, as to the identity of his anonymous friend. But two things are certain—Mrs. Virginia Calvey is a happy woman, and Hank Harper is doing well on a nice two hundred acre farm for which he pays no rent.

8

The Hundred Thousand Dollar Robbery

"I want the whole affair kept unofficial and secret," said Harris, the bank manager.

November Joe nodded. He was seated on the extreme edge of a chair in the manager's private office, looking curiously out of place in that prim, richly furnished room.

"The truth is," continued Harris, "we bankers cannot afford to have our customers' minds unsettled. There are, as you know, Joe, numbers of small depositors, especially in the rural districts, who would be scared out of their seven senses if they knew that this infernal Cecil James Atterson had made off with a hundred thousand dollars. They'd never trust us again."

"A hundred thousand dollars is a wonderful lot of money," agreed Joe.

"Our reserve is over twenty millions, two hundred times a hundred thousand," replied Harris grandiloquently.

Joe smiled in his pensive manner. "That so? Then I guess the bank won't be hurt if Atterson escapes," said he.

"I shall be bitterly disappointed if you permit him to do so," returned Harris. "But here, let's get down to business."

On the previous night, Harris, the manager of the Quebec Branch of the Grand Banks of Canada, had rung me up to borrow November Joe, who was at the time building a log camp for me on one of my properties. I sent Joe a telegram, with the result that within five hours of its receipt he had walked the twenty miles into

108

Quebec, and was now with me at the bank ready to hear Harris's account of the robbery.

The manager cleared his throat and began with a question:—

"Have you ever seen Atterson?"

"No."

"I thought you might have. He always spends his vacations in the woods—fishing, usually. The last two years he has fished Red River. This is what happened. On Saturday I told him to go down to the strong-room to fetch up a fresh batch of dollar and five-dollar bills, as we were short. It happened that in the same safe there was a number of bearer securities. Atterson soon brought me the notes I had sent him for with the keys. That was about noon on Saturday. We closed at one o'clock. Yesterday, Monday, Atterson did not turn up. At first I thought nothing of it, but when it came to afternoon, and he had neither appeared nor sent any reason for his absence, I began to smell a rat. I went down to the strong-room and found that over one hundred thousand dollars in notes and bearer securities were missing.

"I communicated at once with the police and they started to make inquiries. I must tell you that Atterson lived in a boarding-house behind the Frontenac. No one had seen him on Sunday, but on Saturday night a fellow-boarder, called Collings, reports Atterson as going to his room about 10.30. He was the last person who saw him. Atterson spoke to him and said he was off to spend Sunday on the south shore. From that moment Atterson has vanished."

"Didn't the police find out anything further?" inquired Joe.

"Well, we couldn't trace him at any of the railway stations."

"I s'pose they wired to every other police-station within a hundred miles?"

"They did, and that is what brought you into it."

"Why?"

"The constable at Roberville replied that a man answering to the description of Atterson was seen by a farmer walking along the Stoneham road, and heading north, on Sunday morning, early."

"No more facts?"

"No."

"Then let's get back to the robbery. Why are you so plumb sure Atterson done it?"

"The notes and securities were there on Saturday morning."

"How do you know?"

"It's my business to know. I saw them myself."

"Huh! . . . And no one else went down to the strong-room?"

"Only Atterson. The second clerk—it is a rule that no employee may visit the strong-room alone—remained at the head of the stairs, while Atterson descended."

"Who keeps the key?"

"I do."

"And it was never out of your possession?"

"Never."

November was silent for a few moments.

"How long has Atterson been with the bank?"

"Two years odd."

"Anything ag'in' him before?"

"Nothing."

At this point a clerk knocked at the door and, entering, brought in some letters. Harris stiffened as he noticed the writing on one of them. He cut it open and, when the clerk was gone out, he read aloud:—

> Dear Harris,—
>
> I hereby resign my splendid and lucrative position in the Grand Banks of Canada. It is a dog's dirty life; anyway it is so for a man of spirit. You can give the week's screw that's owing to me to buy milk and bath buns for the next meeting of directors.
>
> Yours truly,
>
> C. J. Atterson

"What's the postmark?" asked Joe.

"Rimouski. Sunday, 9.30 A.M."

"It looks like Atterson's the thief," remarked Joe.

"I've always been sure of it!" cried Harris.

"I wasn't," said Joe.

"Are you sure of it now?"

"I'm inclined that way because Atterson had that letter posted by a con—con—what's the word?"

"Confederate?"

"You've got it. He was seen here in town on Saturday at 10.30, and he couldn't have posted no letter in Rimouski in time for the 9.30 A.M. on Sunday unless he'd gone there on the 7 o'clock express on Saturday evening. Yes, Atterson's the thief, all right. And if that really was he they saw Stoneham ways, he's had time to get thirty miles of bush between us and him, and he can go right on till he's on the Labrador. I doubt you'll see your hundred thousand dollars again, Mr. Harris."

"Bah! You can trail him easily enough?"

Joe shook his head. "If you was to put me on his tracks I could," said he, "but up there in the Laurentides he'll sure pinch a canoe and make along a waterway."

"H'm!" coughed Harris. "My directors won't want to pay you two dollars a day for nothing."

"Two dollars a day?" said Joe in his gentle voice. "I shouldn't 'a' thought the two hundred times a hundred thousand dollars could stand a *strain* like that!"

I laughed. "Look here, November, I think I'd like to make this bargain for you."

"Yes, sure," said the young woodsman.

"Then I'll sell your services to Mr. Harris here for five dollars a day if you fail, and ten per cent of the sum you recover if you succeed."

Joe looked at me with wide eyes, but he said nothing.

"Well, Harris, is it on or off?" I asked.

"Oh, on, I suppose, confound you!" said Harris.

November looked at both of us with a broad smile.

Twenty hours later, Joe, a police trooper named Hobson, and I were deep in the woods. We had hardly paused to interview the farmer at Roberville, and then had passed on down the old deserted roads until at last we entered the forest, or, as it is locally called, the "bush."

"Where are you heading for?" Hobson had asked Joe.

"Red River, because if it really was Atterson the farmer saw, I guess he'll have gone up there."

"Why do you think that?"

"Red River's the overflow of Snow Lake, and there is several trappers has canoes on Snow Lake. There's none of them trappers there now in July month, so he can steal a canoe easy. Besides, a man who fears pursuit always likes to get into a country he knows, and you heard Mr. Harris say how Atterson had fished Red River two vacations. Besides" —here Joe stopped and pointed to the ground— "them's Atterson's tracks," he said. "Leastways, it's a black fox to a lynx pelt they are his."

"But you've never seen him. What reason have you . . . ?" demanded Hobson.

"When first we happened on them about four hours back, while you was lightin' your pipe," replied Joe, "they come out of the bush, and when we reached near Carrier's place they went back into the bush again. Then a mile beyond Carrier's out of the bush they come on to the road again. What can that circumventin' mean? Feller who made the tracks don't want to be seen. Number 8 boots, city-made, nails in 'em, rubber heels. Come on."

I will not attempt to describe our journey hour by hour, nor tell how November held to the trail, following it over areas of hard ground and rock, noticing a scratch here and a broken twig there. The trooper, Hobson, proved to be a good track-reader, but he thought himself a better, and, it seemed to me, was a little jealous of Joe's obvious superiority.

We slept that night beside the trail. According to November, the thief was now not many hours ahead of us. Everything depended upon whether he could reach Red River and a canoe before we caught up with him. Still it was not possible to follow a trail in the darkness, so perforce we camped. The next morning November wakened us at daylight and once more we hastened forward.

For some time we followed Atterson's footsteps and then found that they left the road. The police officer went crashing along till Joe stopped him with a gesture.

"Listen!" he whispered.

We moved on quietly and saw that, not fifty yards ahead of us, a man was walking excitedly up and down. His face was quite clear in the slanting sunlight, a resolute face with a small, dark mustache, and a two-days' growth of beard. His head was sunk upon his chest in an attitude of the utmost despair, he waved his hands, and on the still air there came to us the sound of his monotonous muttering.

We crept upon him. As we did so, Hobson leapt forward and, snapping his handcuffs on the man's wrists, cried:—

"Cecil Atterson, I've got you!"

Atterson sprang like a man on a wire, his face went dead white. He stood quite still for a moment as if dazed, then he said in a strangled voice:—

"Got me, have you? Much good may it do you!"

"Hand over that packet you're carrying," answered Hobson.

There was another pause.

"By the way, I'd like to hear exactly what I'm charged with," said Atterson.

"Like to hear!" said Hobson. "You know! Theft of one hundred thousand dollars from the Grand Banks. May as well hand them over and put me to no more trouble!"

"You can take all the trouble you like," said the prisoner.

Hobson plunged his hand into Atterson's pockets, and searched him thoroughly, but found nothing.

"They are not on him," he cried. "Try his pack."

From the pack November produced a square bottle of whiskey, some bread, salt, a slab of mutton—that was all.

"Where have you hidden the stuff?" demanded Hobson.

Suddenly Atterson laughed.

"So you think I robbed the bank?" he said. "I've my own down on them, and I'm glad they've been hit by some one, though I'm not the man. Anyway, I'll have you and them for wrongful arrest with violence."

Then he turned to us. "You two are witnesses."

"Do you deny you're Cecil Atterson?" said Hobson.

"No, I'm Atterson right enough."

"Then look here, Atterson, your best chance is to show us where you've hid the stuff. Your counsel can put that in your favour at your trial."

"I'm not taking any advice just now, thank you. I have said I know nothing of the robbery."

Hobson looked him up and down. "You'll sing another song by and by," he said ironically. "We may as well start in now, Joe, and find where he's cached that packet."

November was fingering over the pack which lay open on the ground, examining it and its contents with concentrated attention. Atterson had sunk down under a tree like a man wearied out.

Hobson and Joe made a rapid examination of the vicinity. A few yards brought them to the end of Atterson's tracks.

"Here's where he slept," said Hobson. "It's all pretty clear. He was dog-tired and just collapsed. I guess that was last night. It's an old camping-place, this." The policeman pointed to weathered beds of balsam and the scars of several camp-fires.

"Yes," he continued, "that's what it is. But the trouble is where has he cached the bank's property?"

For upwards of an hour Hobson searched every conceivable spot, but not so November Joe, who, after a couple of quick casts down to the river, made a fire, put on the kettle, and lit his pipe. Atterson, from under his tree, watched the proceedings with a drowsy lack of interest that struck me as being particularly well simulated.

At length Hobson ceased his exertions, and accepted a cup of the tea Joe had brewed.

"There's nothing cached round here," he said in a voice low enough to escape the prisoner's ear, "and his" —he indicated Atterson's recumbent form with his hand— "trail stops right where he slept. He never moved a foot beyond that nor went down to the river, one hundred yards away. I guess what he's done is clear enough."

"Huh!" said Joe. "Think so?"

"Yep! The chap's either cached them or handed them to an accomplice on the back trail."

"That's so? And what are you going to do next?"

"I'm thinking he'll confess all right when I get him alone." He stood up as November moved to take a cup of tea over to Atterson.

"No, you don't," he cried. "Prisoner Atterson neither eats nor drinks between here and Quebec unless he confesses where he has the stuff hid."

"We'd best be going now," he continued as November, shrugging, came back to the fireside. "You two walk on and let me get a word quiet with the prisoner."

"I'm staying here," said Joe.

"What for?" cried Hobson.

"I'm employed by Bank Manager Harris to recover stolen property," replied Joe.

"But," expostulated Hobson, "Atterson's trail stops right here where he slept. There are no other tracks, so no one could have visited him. Do you think he's got the bills and papers hid about here after all?"

"No," said Joe.

Hobson stared at the answer, then turned to go

"Well," said he, "you take your way and I'll take mine. I reckon I'll get a confession out of him before we reach Quebec. He's a pretty tired man, and he don't rest nor sleep, no, nor sit down, till he's put me wise as to where he hid the stuff he stole."

"He won't ever put you wise," said Joe definitely.

"Why do you say that?"

"'Cause he can't. He don't know himself."

"Bah!" was all Hobson's answer as he turned on his heel.

November Joe did not move as Hobson, his wrist strapped to Atterson's, disappeared down the trail by which we had come.

"Well," I said, "what next?"

"I'll take another look around." Joe leapt to his feet and went quickly over the ground. I accompanied him.

"What do you make of it?" he said at last.

"Nothing," I answered. "There are no tracks nor other signs at all, except these two or three places where old logs have been lying—I expect Atterson picked them up for his fire. I don't understand what you are getting at any more than Hobson does."

"Huh!" said Joe, and led the way down to the river, which, though not more than fifty yards away, was hidden from us by the thick trees.

It was a slow-flowing river, and in the soft mud of the margin I saw, to my surprise, the quite recent traces of a canoe having been beached. Beside the canoe, there was also on the mud the faint mark of a paddle having lain at full length.

Joe pointed to it. The paddle had evidently, I thought, fallen from the canoe, for the impression it had left on the soft surface was very slight.

"How long ago was the canoe here?"

"At first light—maybe between three and four o'clock," replied Joe.

"Then I don't see how it helps you at all. Its coming can't have anything to do with the Atterson robbery, for the distance from here to the camp is too far to throw a packet, and the absence of tracks makes it clear that Atterson cannot have handed the loot over to a confederate in the canoe. Isn't that right?"

"Looks that way," admitted Joe.

"Then the canoe can be only a coincidence."

November shook his head. " I wouldn't go quite so far as to say that, Mr. Quaritch."

Once again he rapidly went over the ground near the river, then returned to the spot where Atterson had slept, following a slightly different track to that by which we had come. Then taking the hatchet from his belt, he split a dead log or two for a fire and hung up the kettle once more. I guessed from this that he had seen at least some daylight in a matter that was still obscure and inexplicable to me.

"I wonder if Atterson has confessed to Hobson yet," I said, meaning to draw Joe.

"He may confess about the robbery, but he can't tell any one where the bank property is."

"You said that before, Joe. You seem very sure of it."

"I am sure. Atterson doesn't know, because he's been robbed in his turn."

"Robbed!" I exclaimed.

Joe nodded.

"And the robber?"

"'Bout five foot six; light-weight; very handsome; has black hair; is, I think, under twenty-five years old; and lives in Lendeville, or near it."

"Joe, you've nothing to go on!" I cried. "Are you sure of this? How can you know?"

"I'll tell you when I've got those bank bills back. One thing's sure—Atterson'll be better off doing five years' hard than if he'd— But here, Mr. Quaritch, I'm going too fast. Drink your tea, and then let us make Lendeville. It's all of eight miles upstream."

It was still early afternoon when we arrived in Lendeville, which could hardly be called a village, except in the Canadian acceptance of that term. It was composed of a few scattered farms and a single general store. Outside one of the farmhouses Joe paused.

"I know the chap that lives in here," he said. "He's a pretty mean kind of a man, Mr. Quaritch. I may find a way to make him talk, though if he thought I wanted information he'd not part with it."

We found the farmer at home, a dour fellow, whose father had emigrated from the north of Scotland half a century earlier.

"Say, McAndrew," began Joe, "there's a chance I'll be bringing a party up on to Red River month after next for the moose-calling. What's your price for hiring two strong horses and a good buckboard to take us and our outfit on from here to the Burnt Lands by Sandy Pond?"

"Twenty dollars."

"Huh!" said Joe, "we don't want to buy the old horses!"

The Scotchman's shaven lips (he wore a chin-beard and whiskers) opened. "It would na' pay to do it for less."

"Then there's others as will."

"And what might their names be?" inquired McAndrew ironically.

"Them as took up Bank-Clerk Atterson when he was here six weeks back."

"Weel, you're wrang!" cried McAndrew, "for Bank-Clerk Atterson juist walked in with young Simon Pointarré and lived with the family at their new mill. So the price is twenty, or I'll nae harness a horse for ye!"

"Then I'll have to go on to Simon Pointarré. I've heard him well spoken of."

"Have ye now? That's queer, for he . . ."

"Maybe, then, it was his brother," said Joe quickly.

"Which?"

"The other one that was with Atterson at Red River."

"There was nae one, only the old man, Simon, and the two girrls."

"Well, anyway, I've got my sportsmen's interests to mind," said November, "and I'll ask the Pointarré's price before I close with yours."

"I'll make a reduce to seventeen dollars if ye agree here and now."

November said something further of Atterson's high regard for Simon Pointarré, which goaded old McAndrew to fury.

"And I'll suppose it was love of Simon that made him employ that family," he snarled. "Oh, yes, that's comic. 'Twas Simon and no that grinning lassie they call Phèdre! . . . Atterson? Tush! I tell ye, if ever a man made a fule o' himself . . ."

But here, despite McAndrew's protests, Joe left the farm.

At the store which was next visited, we learned the position of the Pointarré steading and the fact that old Pointarré, the daughters, Phèdre and Claire, and one son, Simon, were at home, while the other sons were on duty at the mill.

Joe and I walked together along various trails until from a hillside we were able to look down upon the farm, and in a few minutes we were knocking at the door.

It was opened by a girl of about twenty years of age; her bright brown eyes and hair made her very good-looking. Joe gave her a quick glance.

"I came to see your sister," said he.

"Simon," called the girl, "here's a man to see Phèdre."

"What's his business?" growled a man's voice from the inner room.

"I've a message for Miss Pointarré," said Joe.

"Let him leave it with you, Claire," again growled the voice.

"I was to give it to her and no one else," persisted Joe.

This brought Simon to the door. He was a powerful young French-Canadian with up-brushed hair and a dark mustache. He stared at us.

"I've never seen you before," he said at last.

"No, I'm going south and I promised I'd leave a message passing through," replied Joe.

"Who sent you?"

"Can't tell that, but I guess Miss Pointarré will know when I give her the message."

"Well, I suppose you'd best see her. She's down bringing in the cows. You'll find her below there in the meadow"; he waved his arm to where we could see a small stream that ran under wooded hills at a distance of about half a mile. "Yes, you'll find her there below."

Joe thanked him and we set off.

It did not take us long to locate the cows, but there was no sign of the girl. Then, taking up a well-marked trail which led away into the bush, we advanced upon it in silence till, round a clump of pines, it debouched upon a large open shed or byre. Two or three cows stood at the farther end of it, and near them with her back to us was a girl with the sun shining on the burnished coils of her black hair.

A twig broke under my foot and she swung round at the noise.

"What do you want?" she asked.

She was tall and really gloriously handsome.

"I've come from Atterson. I've just seen him," said November.

I fancied her breath caught for the fraction of a second, but only a haughty surprise showed in her face.

"There are many people who see him every day. What of that?" she retorted.

"Not many have seen him to-day, or even yesterday."

Her dark blue eyes were fixed on November. "Is he ill? What do you mean?"

"Huh! Don't they read the newspaper in Lendeville? There's something about him going round. I came thinking you'd sure want to hear," said November.

The colour rose in Phèdre's beautiful face.

"They're saying," went on Joe, "that he robbed the bank where he is employed of a hundred thousand dollars, and instead of trying to get away on the train or by one of the steamers, he made for the woods. That was all right if a Roberville farmer hadn't seen him. So they put the police on his track and I went with the police."

Phèdre turned away as if bored. "What interest have I in this? It *ennuies* me to listen."

"Wait!" replied November. "With the police I went, and soon struck Atterson's trail on the old Colonial Post Road, and in time come up with Atterson himself nigh Red River. The police takes Atterson prisoner and searches him."

"And got the money back!" she said scornfully. "Well, it sounds silly enough. I don't want to hear more."

"The best is coming, Miss Pointarré. They took him but they found nothing. Though they searched him and all roundabout the camp, they found nothing."

"He had hidden it, I suppose."

"So the police thought. And I thought the same, till . . ." (November's gaze never left her face) "till I see his eyes. The pupils were like pin-points in his head." He paused and added, "I got the bottle of whiskey that was in his pack. It'll go in as evidence."

"Of what?" she cried impatiently.

"That Atterson was drugged and the bank property stole from him. You see," continued Joe, "this robbery wasn't altogether Atterson's own idea."

"Ah!"

"No, I guess he had the first notion of it when he was on his vacation six weeks back. . . . He was in love with a wonderful handsome girl. Blue eyes she had and black hair, and her teeth was as good as yours. She pretended to be in love with him, but all along she was in love with—well, I can't say who she was in love with—herself likely. Anyway, I expect she used all her influence to make Atterson rob the bank and then light out for the woods with the stuff. He does all she wants. On his way to the woods she meets him with a pack of food and necessaries. In that pack was a bottle of drugged whiskey. She asks him where he's going to camp that night, he suspects nothing and tells her, and off she goes in a canoe up Red River till she comes to opposite where he's lying drugged. She lands and robs him, but she don't want him to know who done that, so she plays an old game to conceal her tracks. She's a rare active young woman, so she carries out her plan, gets back to her canoe and home to Lendeville. . . . Need I tell any more about her?"

During Joe's story Phèdre's colour had slowly died away.

"You are very clever!" she said bitterly. "But why should you tell me all this?"

"Because I'm going to advise you to hand over the hundred thousand dollars you took from Atterson. I'm in this case for the bank."

"I?" she exclaimed violently. "Do you dare to say that I had anything whatever to do with this robbery, that I have the hundred thousand dollars? . . . Bah! I know nothing about it. How should I?"

Joe shrugged his shoulders. "Then I beg your pardon, Miss Pointarré, and I say goodbye. I must go and make my report to the police and let them act their own way." He turned, but before he had gone more than a step or two, she called to him.

"There is one point you have missed for all your cleverness," she said. "Suppose what you have said is true, may it not be that the girl who robbed Atterson took the money just to return it to the bank?"

"Don't seem to be that way, for she has just denied all knowledge of the property, and denied she had it before two witnesses. Besides, when Atterson comes to know that he's been made a cat's-paw of, he'll be liable to turn King's evidence. No, miss, your only chance is to hand over the stuff—here and now."

"To you!" she scoffed. "And who are you? What right have you . . ."

"I'm in this case for the bank. Old McAndrew knows me well and can tell you my name."

"What is it?"

"People mostly call me November Joe."

She threw back her head—every attitude, every movement of hers was wonderful.

"Now, supposing that the money could be found . . . what would you do?"

"I'd go to the bank and tell them I'd make shift to get every cent back safe for them if they'd agree not to prosecute . . . anybody."

"So you are man enough not to wish to see me in trouble?"

November looked at her. "I was sure not thinking of you at all," he said simply, "but of Bank-Clerk Atterson, who's lost the girl he robbed for and ruined himself for. I'd hate to see that chap over-punished with a dose of gaol too. . . . But the bank people only wants their money, and I guess if they get that they'll be apt to think the less said about the robbery the better. So if you take my advice—why, now's the time to see old McAndrew. You see, Miss Pointarré, I've got the cinch on you."

She stood still for a while. "I'll see old man McAndrew," she cried suddenly. "I'll lead. It's near enough this way."

Joe turned after her, and I followed. Without arousing McAndrew's suspicions, Joe satisfied the girl as to his identity.

Before dark she met us again. "There!" she said, thrusting a packet into Joe's hand. "But look out for yourself! Atterson isn't the only man who'd break the law for love of me. Think of that at night in the lonely bush!"

I saw her sharp white teeth grind together as the words came from between them.

"My!" ejaculated November looking after her receding figure, "she's a bad loser, ain't she, Mr. Quaritch?"

We went back into Quebec, and Joe made over to the bank the amount of their loss as soon as Harris, the manager, agreed (rather against his will) that no questions should be asked nor action taken.

The same evening I, not being under the same embargo regarding questions, inquired from Joe how in the world the fair Phèdre covered her tracks from the canoe to where Atterson was lying.

"That was simple for an active girl. She walked ashore along the paddle, and after her return to the canoe threw water upon the mark it made in the mud. Didn't you notice how faint it was?"

"But when she got on shore—how did she hide her trail then?"

"It's not a new trick. She took a couple of short logs with her in the canoe. First she'd put one down and step onto it, then she'd put the other one farther and step onto that. Next she'd lift the one behind, and so on. Why did she do that? Well, I reckon she thought the trick good enough to blind Atterson. If he'd found a woman's tracks after being robbed, he'd have suspected."

"But you said before we left Atterson's camp that whoever robbed him was middle height, a light weight, and had black hair."

"Well, hadn't she? Light weight because the logs wasn't much drove into the ground, not tall since the marks of them was so close together."

"But the black hair?"

Joe laughed. "That was the surest thing of the lot, and put me wise to it and Phèdre at the start. Twisted up in the buckle of the pack she gave Atterson I found several strands of splendid black hair. She must've caught her hair in the buckles while carrying it."

"But, Joe, you also said at Red River that the person who robbed Atterson was not more than twenty-five years old?"

"Well, the hair proved it was a woman, and what but being in love with her face would make a slap-up bank-clerk like Atterson have any truck with a settler's girl? And them kind are early ripe and go off their looks at twenty-five. I guess, Mr. Quaritch, her age was a pretty safe shot."

9

THE LOOTED ISLAND

It was a clear night, bright with stars. Joe and I were sitting by our camp-fire near one of the fjords of western Alaska, where we had gone on a hunting expedition after the great moose of the West.

I was talking, when suddenly Joe touched me.

"Shsh!" he whispered. "There's some feller moving down by the creek."

"Impossible!" I said. "Why, we're a hundred miles from—"

"He's coming this way." Joe rose and motioned me back among the shadows. "There's some queer folk round here, I guess. Best be taking no chances."

We waited, and I was soon aware of a figure advancing through the night.

Then a voice said, "Fine night, mates," and a sinewy, long-armed fellow, with a bushy red beard, stepped into the circle of light.

"The cold makes you keep your hands in your pockets, don't it?" said Joe gently. "It does me."

I then noticed that both men were covering each other with revolvers through their pockets. The stranger slowly drew out his hand.

"Let's talk," said he sourly. "Who are you?"

"Give us a lead," said Joe.

"I'm John Stafford."

"This here is Mr. Quaritch, of Quebec. I'm his guide. We're come after big game."

Stafford looked round the camp with a shrewd eye.

"I guess you're speaking truth. It's up to me to apologize," he said.

He held out his hand, which November Joe and I shook with gravity.

"I'm free to own I was doubtful about you," he said. "You'll understand that when I tell you what's happened."

"Huh!" said Joe. "Sit down. There's tea in the kettle."

Stafford helped himself.

"Perhaps," he said at length, "you've noticed an island about eight miles off the coast, lying nor'-nor'-west?"

"Sort of loaf-shaped island? Yes."

"That's where I come from—Eel Island. I have a fox farm there. I returned to it yesterday after a run down to Valdez. When I went away a fortnight ago, I left my man in charge of some of the finest black foxes between this and Ungava. I got back to find the foxes all killed and my hired man gone—disappeared."

"Who was he?"

"An Aleut, called Sam. He's been in my employ three years. I see what you're thinking—that he killed the foxes, and I'd have thought that myself, only I know he didn't."

"How's that?"

"One reason is that I own only one boat, and when I went to the mainland last Friday week I took it, leaving Sam on the island. It's all of seven miles from the coast, so he couldn't have got away if he wanted. That, I say, is one reason why it couldn't have been him. The other reason's as good. I was decoyed away so cleverly. Here's the letter that did it."

The fox-farmer drew out a crumpled sheet of ruled paper from his pocket and handed it to me. I read aloud:—

> Sir,—Your wife wants you to come down at once. She's due for an operation in the hospital here on Friday week, and she's hard put to it to plan for the children till she gets about again. So you'd best come. Yours truly,
>   S. Macfarlane,
>   (*Doctor*).

I gave him back the letter. "Any man would have gone on such news," I said.

"Well, I did," said Stafford savagely, "but it was a bad bit o' work. I got that letter twelve days back, and off I went hot-foot, leaving Aleut Sam in charge. It took me a week going down. When I reached the house where my wife is living, she was surprised to see me, and I showed her the letter. . . . You can guess. . . . It was all a plant! There wasn't any Dr. Macfarlane, nor any operation. You might have struck me down when I heard that, but it wasn't long before I dropped to the game, and back I came—record-breaking travel—to Eel Island. . . . I found the place clean gutted. All the blacks and silvers caught and killed, and the skinned carcasses lying around. And Aleut Sam vanished as if he had never lived."

"Have you a notion who done it?" inquired November.

Stafford ground his teeth. "It may have been done for spite, but whoever he was he lived in my cabin several days, and slept in my bunk. . . . I wonder what he did with Sam. Knocked him on the head and heaved him in the sea like as not."

Joe nodded.

Stafford continued: "I could tell he hadn't been long gone, and so when I saw the smoke of your camp-fire, I got the skiff and came over. I thought it might be the chap that raided my farm. That's why I walked up with my revolver in my fist. . . . I'm nigh desperate. The work of three years gone . . . three winters spent with Sam alone, like some kind of a Crusoe and his man Friday . . . and keeping my wife and two little gals down at Valdez . . ."

"Look here, ain't it a bit early in the year to kill foxes?" said Joe, after a pause.

"They'd have been worth twenty-five per cent more in a month."

"Then why. . .?"

"Because I couldn't have been decoyed away except while the steamer was running before the winter closed down. See?"

"O' course," said Joe. "And you think some one done it for spite?"

Stafford bent nearer.

"This dirty business may have been done as much for gain as spite. Even as early as this in the year the pelts were worth fifteen thousand dollars."

"My!" said Joe. "Suspect any one in particular?"

"I believe it may have been Trapper Simpson. He's had a down on me this good while back. Well, if it was him, he's paid me out good, the blackguard . . . the . . ."

"Hard words don't bring down nor man nor deer," said Joe.

There was a silence; then I said:—

"What would you give the man that discovered who it was robbed you?"

"If he didn't get me back my pelts, I could give him nothing. If he did, he'd be welcome to five hundred dollars," replied the fox-farmer.

"Good enough, November?" I asked.

Joe nodded.

"What do you mean?" asked Stafford, turning to Joe. "You a trail-reader?"

"Learnin' to be," said Joe.

Thus it was agreed that we should go across to Eel Island at dawn to let November have a look round. I could see that Stafford had no great belief in the chances of Joe's success—which was not unnatural seeing that he knew nothing of November's powers.

We were away in good time. There was only a glimmer in the east when we got aboard the fox-farmer's skiff, and soon we were crossing the bar of the estuary. Just as we passed beyond it, Eel Island showed through the morning mists. As we approached, I saw that it was a barren atoll without any sign of human tenant. We made a good passage, and in due time, with our visitor at the tiller and November at the mainsheet, we ran into a poor anchorage.

We went ashore, and Joe at once took a cast, looking for tracks, though he knew he was little likely to find any, for the ground was as hard as iron and had been impervious for days. This was a state of affairs which particularly interested me, since hitherto most of

Joe's successes that I had witnessed had owed a good deal to the reading of trails. In the present case this seemed impossible, for the frost had held from before the date of the crime.

We next climbed to Stafford's cabin. It proved to be built of wood with a felt roof, and the structure crouched in the lee of a gigantic boulder on the one side, and of the shoulder of a ridge on the other.

The owner threw open the door.

"Come right in," said he.

"Wait!" said Joe. "You told us the robber lived in here while he was on the island. If things is the way he left them, I'd like to look round."

"Have your way," said Stafford. "I haven't disturbed them. I put off directly I saw your smoke, and I hadn't been long ashore."

Joe went in and made a rapid examination of the cabin. It was a tiny place furnished only with a rough deal table, a chair cut from a barrel, and the usual shallow wooden tray for a bunk. The walls were decorated with smaller shelves on which were heaped provisions, a few books, cooking-pots, knives, forks, and plates, all helter-skelter.

November examined everything with his usual swift care. He lit match after match and peered about the stove, for the interior of the cabin was pretty dark even in the daytime.

After this he bent over the table and, drawing his knife, scratched at a stain on the near side, and then at a similar stain upon the other.

"I'm through," he said at length.

Stafford, who had been watching Joe's proceedings with an air of incredulity that bordered on derision, now stepped forward and cast his eyes rapidly over every spot where Joe had paused, then turned sharply to question him:—

"Found out anything?"

"Not much," answered Joe.

"Well, all I can see is that the villain has eaten a good share of my grub."

"I dare say," said Joe. "There was two of them, you know . . ."

"No, I don't! And what else can you tell me about them?"

"I think they was man and wife. She's a smallish woman; I'd guess she's maybe weakly, too. And he's fond of reading; anyway, he can read."

Stafford stared at November half suspiciously.

"What?" he shouted. "Are you kidding me? Or how did you get all that?"

"That's easy," replied November. "There are two or three traces of a little flat foot in front of the stove, and a woman couldn't run this job on her own, so it's likely there was a man, too."

Stafford grunted. "You said she was weakly!"

"I thought maybe she was, for if she hadn't spilt the water out of the kettle most times she took it off the stove there wouldn't be any track, and here is one near on top of the other, so it happened more'n once on the same spot. She found your kettle heavy, Mr. Stafford," Joe said seriously.

"I'm free to own that seems sense," acknowledged Stafford. "But the reading—that's different."

"Table's been pulled up alongside the bunk, see that scrape of the leg; and he's had the lamp close up alongside near the edge where the stain is. There's plenty old oil-stains in the middle of the table, but these close to the edges ain't been long on—you can see that for yourself."

"By Jingo!" said the fox-farmer. "Anything else?"

"The chap what robbed you was a trapper all right, and had killed a red fox recent, so recent he carried it across and skinned it here."

"Where?"

"By your stove." Joe bent down and picked up some short, red hairs. "Clumsy skinning!" said he. "Let's go out and take a look round the island."

Stafford led the way. At a short distance some of the skinned carcasses lay. They were blackened by the weather, and lay open to the sky, looking as horrible as skinned carcasses always will. Joe turned them over. Suddenly he bent down with that quick intentness that I had learnt to connect with his more important discoveries. From one he passed to another, till he had handled every carcass.

"What is it?" asked Stafford, whose respect for Joe was visibly increasing with each moment.

November straightened his back. "I'm sure it weren't done for spite," he remarked.

"What do you mean?"

But Joe would say nothing more. So we passed on, climbing all over the island. Stafford pointed out another lying some five miles north where he told us he kept his less valuable stock.

"There's a lot of red and cross foxes over there on Edith Island (it's named for my eldest gal)," he said. "Whenever there happens a black one in the litters I try to catch it, and bring it over here to Eel— Hullo! What's that?"

Stafford stood with his hands shading his eyes, staring at Edith Island.

"Look! That's smoke or I'm dreaming," he cried.

A very faint line of bluish haze rose from the distant rock.

"Smoke it is," said Joe.

"But the island is uninhabited. Come on! Come on!" cried Stafford excitedly. "It may be those ruffians clearing out Edith Island, too. We'll get after them!"

"All right, Mr. Stafford," agreed Joe. "But, look here, it *may* be those chaps that robbed you, but I don't want you to run up against disappointment. I guess it's liable to be your Aleut Sam marooned over there."

"Why?"

"That's a signal fire. Whoever's made that fire is putting on moss. And I've noticed things here that make me think it ain't likely they killed Sam."

"Let's get after them, anyway," cried Stafford. "If it's Sam, he'll be able to help us with his story."

It was not long before we were once more in the boat and tacking across towards Edith Island. As we drew nearer the volume of smoke grew thicker.

"It's sure a signal smoke," said Joe. "The feller's putting on wet moss."

The wind served us fairly well, and, as we ran under the lee of the land, we were aware of a figure standing on the beach waiting for us.

"It's Aleut Sam, sure enough," said Stafford.

The Aleut proved to be a squat fellow of a most Mongolian cast of countenance. A few score of long hairs, distinct, thick, and black, made up his mustache. His beard was even scantier, and a tight cap of red wool which he wore showed off the umber tint of his large round face.

We rowed ashore in the canvas boat, and on the beach Stafford held a rapid conversation with his man in Indian. Neither Joe nor I could follow what was said, but presently Stafford enlightened us.

"Sam says that one night, four days after I left Eel Island, he had just eaten his supper when he heard a knocking on the door. Thinking it must be me who had returned, he opened it. Seeing no one, he stepped out into the dark, when a pair of arms were thrown round him, and a cloth that smelt like the stuff that made him go asleep in the hospital (Sam's had most of his toes off on account of frost-bite down to Valdez) was clapped about his head. He struggled, and the next thing he knew he felt very sick, and when he came to, he found himself tied up and lying in the bottom of a boat at sea. He could tell there were two men with him. He thinks he was about half an hour conscious, when one of them, with his face muffled, stopped sculling, and knelt on his chest and put the sweet-smelling cloth over his head a second time. After that he does not remember any more until he woke up on the beach here. It was still dark, and the men and boat were gone. He was very sick again, and for all that night and most of the next day he thought he was going to die.

"Towards evening he began to feel better, and, wandering about, discovered a barrel of dried fish which had been tumbled ashore from the boat which marooned him—to keep him from starving, I suppose. He went up into the scrub and made a fire. Since then he's been here and seen no one. That's all."

"Then he didn't ever really see the faces of the chaps that kidnapped him?"

Stafford translated the question to Sam and repeated the answer.

"One had a beard and was a big man; he wore a peaked cap. Anything else to ask him?"

"Yes. How long has he been here on this island?"

"Eight days."

"What's he been doing all the time?"

"Just wandering around."

"Where has he been camped?"

Stafford raised his thumb over his shoulder. "In the scrub above here."

Joe nodded. "Well, let's go to his camping-place and boil the kettle. He'll sure have a bit of fire there."

So we made our way up through the scrub, filling the kettle from a little spring on the way as the Aleut led us to his bivouac. While I looked about it, I wondered once more at the skill of the men of the wilderness.

A rough break-wind masked the fire, and above the sleeping-place the boughs of dwarf willow and spruce were interlaced in cunning fashion.

Joe stirred the smouldering logs into life, but in doing so was so unfortunate as to overturn the kettle.

"That's bad," said he. "Best tell your man to get some more water."

Stafford sent off Sam on his errand; but no sooner had the Aleut disappeared than November was on his knees examining the charred embers and delving among the ashes. It was easy to see that he was hot on some scent, though what on earth it could be neither Stafford nor I had any notion. After some busy moments he drew back.

"Get rid of your hired man for a while longer, only so he don't suspect anything," he said. "I hear him coming."

"You mean he's in the robbery?"

"He sure is. And, what's more, it looks to me like he's your only chance of getting your foxes back. Here he comes."

A moment later Sam appeared in sight walking up the narrow track between the rocks, kettle in hand. Stafford spoke to him in Aleut. Sam grunted in acquiescence, and went off up the hill that formed the centre of the island.

"I told him to go gather some more wood while the kettle's boiling. Now you can talk and tell me who you think has the pelts of my foxes."

"No one hasn't," replied Joe.

"What!"

"Your foxes ain't dead."

"Ain't dead? You've forgot their skinned carcasses!"

"I allow we saw *some* skinned carcasses, but they was the carcasses of red foxes worth no more than ten dollars apiece instead of a thousand."

"But—"

"I know you took it for sure they was your foxes—and you're a fox-farmer, and ought to know. But I examined those carcasses mighty careful. Their eyes wasn't the right colour for black foxes. That's one thing. For another, I found some red hairs. It ain't in nature you can take a pelt off and not a hair stick on the body under."

Stafford digested this in silence.

"But why in creation should the chaps have taken the trouble to bring over red fox carcasses?" he inquired at length.

"That's easy answered. They was after your best for stock. It's pretty likely they didn't take them far, and they wouldn't want you nosing about for your live foxes."

"Is that it?"

"Another thing, the robbers was six days or more on Eel Island. Now, they could catch and kill all your foxes in two. But to catch them so they wouldn't be hurt would take time. No, your foxes ain't dead yet; and they ain't far off, neither, and your Aleut knows who's got them."

"Why are you so sure about him being in it?"

"He told you he'd been eight days on this island, didn't he?"

Stafford nodded. "Eight days, that's what he said."

"He lied. I knew it the moment I set eyes on his fire."

Stafford frowned down at the singing kettle.

Joe continued:—

"Not enough ash to this fire to make heat to keep a man without a blanket comfortable for eight days this weather. And look! the boughs he's broke off for his bed. They're too fresh. Ag'in, he ain't got no axe here, yet the charred ends of the thicker bits on the fire has been cut with an axe. It's clear as light. The robbers ferried Sam across here about two days back, cut some wood for him so he shouldn't be too cold, gave him grub to last till 'bout the time you'd likely be home, and left him."

"I guess you're right. I see it now. I'm grateful to you."

Joe shook his head. "Keep that a bit till we've got your foxes back; and it looks to me like it might be a difficult proposition to prove who done it, unless o' course we could persuade Sam—"

"I'll persuade him. There he is coming over the hill."

"I wonder if your Sam is a fighter?" said Joe. "Anyway, best not be too venturesome. He's got a knife."

Stafford reached for his rifle, but Joe intervened.

"Stay you still and I'll show you the way we do in the lumber-camps."

Sam's strong, squat figure advanced towards us. As he stooped to throw the wood he had brought on the ground, Joe caught his shoulder with one hand and snatched the knife from his belt with the other. And then there flashed across the features of the Aleut an expression like a mad dog's; he flung himself gnashing and snarling on November.

But he was in the grip of a man too strong for him, and, though he returned again and again to the attack, the huge young woodsman twisted him to earth, where Stafford and I tied his struggling limbs.

This done, we rolled him over.

"Now," said Stafford, "who is it has got my foxes?"

The Aleut shook his head.

Stafford pulled out his revolver, opened the breech, made sure it was loaded, and cocked it. Next he held his watch in front of

Sam's face and pointed out the fact that it wanted but five minutes to the hour.

"I'm telling him if he don't confess," he said, "I'll shoot him when the hand reaches the hour." He turned to us: "You'd best go."

"Good Heavens! you don't really mean—" I cried.

Stafford winked. Joe and I went down to the beach below.

A quarter of an hour passed before Stafford joined us.

"What's happened?" I asked.

"He's confessed all right." Then Stafford looked at Joe. "It all went through just the way you said. It was a rival fox-farmer, Jurgensen, did it. Landed on Eel Island with his wife the night I left, they were there until two days ago; took them all their time, and Sam's, to get my foxes. Then they brought him over here. Yes, Mr. Joe, you've been right from start to finish."

"What's going to be done next?"

"There's two courses. One is to put things in the hands of the police; the other is to sail right along with this wind to Upsala Island, where the Jurgensens live. But I can't go there alone. It's a nasty sort of business, you see, and one that shouldn't be carried through without witnesses, and I feel I've cut a big slice out of your hunting already."

"I don't know what Mr. Quaritch thinks," said Joe, "but perhaps he'd like to be in at the finish."

"Of course," said I.

And now I will leave out any account of the events of the next sixteen hours, which we spent in the skiff, and pick up the thread of this history again with Stafford knocking at the door of the Jurgensens' cabin on Upsala Island. We had landed there after dark.

Joe and I stood back while Stafford faced the door. It was thrown open, and a big, ginger-bearded Swede demanded his business.

"I've just called around to take back my foxes," said Stafford.

"Vot voxes?"

"The blacks and silvers you stole."

"You are madt!"

"Shut it!" cried Stafford. "Ten days ago you and your wife, having decoyed me away to Valdez, went to Eel Island. You were there eight days, during which time you cleaned out every animal I owned on it. I know you didn't kill them, though you tried to make me believe you had by leaving the skinned carcasses of a lot of red foxes. Three days ago you left Eel Island . . ."

As he spoke I saw the wizened figure of a woman squeezing out under the big Swede's elbow. She had a narrow face with blinking, malevolent eyes, that she fixed on Stafford.

"Zo! Vot then?" jeered Jurgensen.

"Then you rowed over to Edith Island and marooned my man, Aleut Sam, who was in the robbery with you."

The big Swede snatched up a rifle by the door and stepped out.

"Get out of here," he cried, "or—" He paused on catching sight of Joe and myself.

"I'll go if you wish it," said Stafford dangerously. "But if I do it'll be to return with the police."

"And look here, Mr. Dutchman," broke in Joe gently, "if it comes to that you'll get put away for a fifteen years' rest cure, sure."

"Who are you?" bellowed Jurgensen.

"He's the man that told me your wife was weakly and spilled the water from the kettle when she lifted it, for he found her tracks at my place by the stove. He's the man that discovered axe-cut log-ends in Aleut Sam's fire on Edith Island, when we knew Sam had no axe with him. He's the man I owe a lot to."

"Me alzo," said Jurgensen venomously as he bowed his head. "Vot you vant—your terms?" he asked at last.

Stafford had his answer ready. "My own foxes—that's restoration, and two of yours by way of interest—that's retribution."

"Ant if I say no?"

"You won't. Where's my foxes?"

Jurgensen hesitated, but clearly there could be only one decision in the circumstances. "I haf them in my kennels," he answered.

"Wire enclosures?" cried Stafford in disgust.

"Yess."

"You can't grow a decent pelt in a cage," snapped Stafford, with the eagerness of a fanatic mounted upon his hobby. "You must let them live their natural life as near as possible or their colour suffers. The pigmentary glands get affected—"

"Poof! I haf read of all that in the book, 'Zientific Zelection of Colour Forms.'"

"Yes," put in Joe. "You read a good bit while you were at Mr. Stafford's place, that's so? Lying in Mr. Stafford's bunk?"

Jurgensen raised startled eyes. "You see me?"

"No."

"How you know, then?"

Joe laughed. "I guess the spiders must 'a' told me," said he.

10
The Mystery of Fletcher Buckman

I was dozing. It seemed to me deep in the night. The train that November Joe and I had boarded late the previous evening on our return from a trip in Quebec was passing, with a rattle and a roar, between the woods which flank the metals, when suddenly there rang out shriek upon shriek, such as mark the top note of grief and human horror.

Upon the instant the whole sleeping-car awoke; half a dozen passengers sprang to the carpeted floor, surprise and consternation eloquent in their faces and attitudes.

"It's from that private car," cried some one. "Who's in it?"

A bearded man answered: "Fletcher Buckman and his wife."

"It was a woman's scream."

"We must see what's wrong."

The bearded man and two others ran down the corridor, and at that moment the conductor stepped inside the door and confronted them squarely.

"What's happened?" gasped a voice. "There's murder doing. Here, let's pass!"

The conductor's hard face checked them. "Bah! Mrs. Buckman's had a nightmare. That's all there's to it," he said roughly.

I knew that his words were mere invention. His next act made me even more certain, for he locked the door behind him, walked quickly through the car, paying no attention to the babble of questions, remonstrance, incredulity, and advice thrust upon him from all sides; and a minute later he reappeared with November Joe, who, scorning sleepers, was travelling in the car ahead.

As he passed, Joe whispered, "Come on." I followed, hastily pulling on my coat, for I had lain down dressed. We stepped out from the blaze of electricity into a cold, white light of dawn, against which the massed trees on either side loomed black and wet as the train steamed forward.

On the open platform between the cars the conductor said a few words to Joe: "I brought you along, November, for I want a witness, anyway."

Then we passed into electricity again as we entered the private car. It would be impossible to forget the sight that met us. Across the floor lay the figure of a woman; her face, showing out among folds of shining silk, was white as chalk, and, though she had lost consciousness, it was still drawn with terror.

But my eyes passed by her to the side of the car, where, close to the bed-place, the body of a man was dangling, hung by the neck to a stout brass hook.

I could see that he was thinnish, with a drooping mustache and outrageously bald. He lurched and swayed to the swaying of the train, but it was the dreadful pink head bobbing stiffly that lent the last touch of horror. He was dressed in orange-coloured pyjamas, and his bare heels beat a tattoo against the side-boarding of the bunk.

In a second we had cut him down; but as the rigid body sank its weight upon our arms, we knew that life must have left it some good while before.

"It's Fletch Buckman, sure enough," said the conductor; "and he's had time to stiffen. No hope, I reckon! . . . There's no doc on the cars, but we can get a couple of women to see to Mrs. Buckman. We'll start to carry her out of this right now, before she comes to."

The conductor and I raised her in our arms, and within two minutes we had left her in kindly hands.

When we got back Joe was still engrossed in his examination of the body. He put up his hand to warn us back as we appeared at the door.

"Wait a bit," he said. "You can talk from there, Steve. You were saying—"

The conductor took up what was evidently the thread of the story he had been telling to Joe when he first called him. "As I was explaining to you, I heard the screech and looked in just as she dropped. I stepped over and got at Fletch, but I knew by the feel of him it was too late to try any reviving. Next I went for you—" He paused.

Joe made no reply.

"She slept in the little compartment beyond 'cause he always stayed up half the night working, and often slept in the bunk here, like he did to-night," continued the conductor. "Guess it's suicide, Joe." He was leaning forward and looking into the contorted dead face on the pillow of the bed.

"Come in now," said November abruptly, and passed into Mrs. Buckman's sleeping-room, from which a door opened to the rear platform of the car. While he was busy moving in and out, Steve, the conductor, went round, making his own observations.

And here I may as well give a slight description of the car. It was not a large one, but was comfortably fitted with a couple of armchairs and the bunk already mentioned. A rolled-up hammock for use in the hot weather was strapped against the panelling, and the hook which had upheld poor Buckman's body was intended for supporting one end of this hammock when slung.

To the left was an office bureau with writing materials upon it, also a typewriter and an open leather bag containing folded papers. There were windows on both sides of the car; but while the one on the left was still covered with its slatted shutter, the glass of the opposite windows was bare, and showed the dark night-cloud sinking in the west.

Steve uttered an exclamation, and I saw he was reading some words typed on a sheet of paper fixed in the machine. November, who was still standing by the side of the dead man, looked round. Steve crossed over to him.

"It's sure suicide," he said; "though what made him do it, and he already a millionaire and likely to be richer every day, beats me!"

"Suicide," repeated Joe softly. "Why suicide?"

"That's his own belt he was hung up with," replied Steve; "there's his name on it. And better proof than that you'll find on the typewriter over there. You can read it for yourselves."

I joined Joe at the table. The upper part of the sheet of paper, which was still in the machine, held some nine or ten lines of a business letter; then, an inch or more below, a few words stood out upon the plain whiteness:—

"*Heaven help me! I can bear it no longer!*"

"That's the sort of slush they mostly write when they're waiting to jump off the edge of the world," remarked the conductor. "That settles it."

"That's so," said Joe. "Only it wasn't Buckman wrote that."

"Who else could it be?"

"The man that hanged him."

The conductor gave a snort of laughter.

"Then you surmise that some one came in here and hanged Fletch Buckman?"

"Just that."

"O' course, Buckman consented to being hung!" jeered Steve.

"Buckman was dead *before* he was hung!" said November.

"What's that you're saying?" cried Steve.

"If you examine the body—" began Joe.

The conductor made a forward movement, but Joe caught his arm.

"Let's see the soles of your boots before you get tramping about too much. Steady, hold on to the table. Now!"

He studied the upturned sole for a minute.

"Huh!" said he. "Now come over to the body. Look at the throat. There is the mark of a belt. But see here." He indicated some roundish, livid bruises. "No strap ever made those. Those were made by a man's fingers. Buckman was throttled by a pair of mighty strong hands."

Steve looked obstinate.

"But he was hanging!" he argued.

"When he was dead, the murderer slung him up with his own belt. I expect he remembered the notion of suicide would come in convenient to give him a start, anyhow, so the man went to the typewriter and printed out those words. It was a right cute trick, and it came wonderful near serving its turn," Joe paused.

Steve raised an altered face.

"It's a cinch, I'm afraid," he admitted. "And a durned mean thing for me. The company'll fire me over this."

"When did you last see Buckman alive?" inquired Joe.

"At midnight. Just before we passed Silent Water Siding."

"Was he alone?"

"He was then; Mrs. Buckman had gone to bed. But he had been talking to a fellow 'bout half an hour before that—a man with a beard. I don't know his name."

"He's still on the cars; we haven't stopped since."

"Sure."

"Then he can wait while—"

November was not destined to say more just then. The door behind us was wrenched open, and Mrs. Buckman stood there. At her shoulder I could see the peering faces of the women who had been attending on her.

"I tell you he was murdered, murdered!" she cried. "This talk of suicide is folly. He would never have killed himself—never!"

She was wild with grief, but the terror had gone from her face; she had only one thought now—to avenge her husband. And, indeed, she made a tragic figure—a slight woman, no longer young, held by sheer will against the shock of the hideous blow Fate had dealt her.

"Poor dear! Poor dear! She don't know what she's saying," murmured one of the women.

"Be silent! I do know! I tell you that my husband has been murdered. Won't any of you believe me?" She wrung her hands, clenching her fingers together. "Won't one of you believe me?"

November stepped forward.

"I do, ma'am," he said. "I've been looking—"

She made an effort to master herself.

"Tell me what you've seen. Don't spare me. He's dead, and all that is left to do is to find who killed him! It was murder! You know that."

"There's plenty signs of it," said Joe gently. "I was just going to look round, but perhaps you might care to answer me a few questions first?"

"Ask me anything! But, oh, send away those people!"

Joe glanced at Steve.

"Lock the door, and don't let anything be touched or disturbed," he said; then he led Mrs. Buckman into the farther compartment, away from the sight of the poor shape upon the bunk.

In a second he made a comfortable seat for her, but she would not take it; her whole body and soul seemed absorbed in the single desire.

"What have you to ask me?"

"Just what brought you and Mr. Buckman here. Where were you going? Where have you come from? And what are your suspicions? The whole story, whatever you can think of, nothing is too trifling."

In terse, rapid sentences, Mrs. Buckman gave us the following facts:—

"You have probably heard the name of Buckman before. Most people have. My husband was one of the greatest and most trusted oil experts in the States. He had large holdings in the Giant Oil Company. About a fortnight ago a situation developed which made it necessary for him to leave New York and come down to the Tiger Lily Oilfield. The Giant Company were thinking of buying it, or rather of buying a controlling interest in it. Before doing so they wanted a first-hand opinion, and it was suggested that my husband should travel down to look into the matter."

She glanced at November's intent face, and went on:—

"Perhaps you know that this line runs close to the Tiger Lily Eastern Section, so we had our private car attached and came along. That was on Thursday, a week ago. We had the car run onto a siding, and all the days since my husband has been hard at work. He finished the day before yesterday, but as there was no express earlier than this evening, we waited for it and just before dark our car was linked to this train.

"We dined together, and after dinner a man, Knowles, who was on the train, sent in to ask my husband to see him. My husband was much annoyed, for it appeared that Knowles had been manager of a large retail depot, from which he had been dismissed for some carelessness. However, my husband made it a rule to give personal interviews whenever he could, and he ordered Knowles to be sent along. As soon as he appeared, I went away, but I saw he was a big, sour-looking man in shabby clothes.

"I came into this compartment and began to read. For a good while only the murmur of their talking reached me, then a voice was raised, and I caught some words distinctly: 'You won't put me back? Think! I have a wife and children!' It was Knowles speaking. 'It is impossible, as you know,' said my husband. 'Giant Oil never reconsiders a decision.' 'Then look out for yourself!' Knowles shouted, and I at once opened the door. I was terrified, the man looked so threatening and bitter; but the instant I appeared he whipped round and went out of the car."

"Did Mr. Buckman tell you anything more about him?"

"Not much," she answered, with a sort of trembling breath, "for he was a little annoyed that I should have come in when I heard Knowles angry. But that was soon forgotten, and we sat talking for about an hour. At ten, as I was feeling tired, I said I would go to bed. My husband told me he had work to do which would keep him another couple of hours, and he would sleep in here so as not to disturb me."

"Do you know what work it was?"

"Yes, it was his report on the Tiger Lily Oilfield."

"The report that was to decide whether the Giant people would buy it or not?"

She made a movement of assent.

"I suppose it would have been worth a great deal to certain people if they could have found out the nature of that report?" said Joe.

"My husband told me that any one who could get knowledge of it in time could make a fortune."

"Can you tell me just how?"

"My husband explained that to me one day while we were down at the Tiger Lily. A month ago the shares of the Tiger Lily stood at eight dollars, but when rumours got about that the Giant Company meant to buy it they rose to twelve dollars, which is about the price they stand at to-day. My husband said that if his report were favourable the shares would jump to twenty, or even thirty, but that if it were unfavourable they would, of course, sink very low, indeed."

"I understand."

Mrs. Buckman went on: "Even I knew nothing of whether his decision was for or against the purchase. He never told me business secrets in case I should inadvertently let slip some information. I have no idea what line his report was to take."

"Was it not rather strange that Mr. Buckman should delay the writing of the report to the last moment? You have been days on the siding, and you tell me he had all the information ready the day before yesterday, and that you were only waiting for the express; yet he postponed writing his report until actually travelling late at night?" inquired November.

"I can explain that," replied Mrs. Buckman. "In his life my husband has had to deal with many secrets of great commercial value, so many that secrecy had become second nature with him, and it was one of his invariable rules never to put anything into writing until the last possible moment."

"There's reason in that," said Joe. "And now, did you hear anything after you went to bed?"

"I heard my husband working on the typewriter until I fell asleep. When I awoke I fancied I heard him moving about, and I called to him to go to bed. He did not answer, and as all was quiet I fell asleep again. If I had only got up then, I might have saved him!" She hid her face in her hands, but after a minute she mastered her emotion. "The next time I started up in a fright and turned on the light. It was long past three. I snatched at my wrapper and rushed into the next compartment. You know what I saw."

"One more question, ma'am, and then I'll trouble you no more. Have you any feeling as to who could have done this?" asked Joe, after a short silence.

"I don't know what to say—Knowles looked a desperate man. I heard his threat. But who are you, and why—"

Steve, who had hung in the doorway while this conversation was going on, now interposed to explain Joe, but she hardly seemed to heed. Before he concluded she put both her hands on November's arm.

"Remember, I'll spend the last cent I possess if you will only find that man! What are you going to do first?"

"I must examine the car. I haven't had time to do that thoroughly yet," said Joe. "But wait a minute. Look through his bag and see if the report of the Tiger Lily is in it."

It was not to be found. And after that, Steve took Mrs. Buckman away, for now that the strain of telling her story was over, she seemed as if she would collapse.

"There's a woman for you!" exclaimed Joe. "Say, Mr. Quaritch, I'll hunt that man for her till he drops in his tracks!"

Joe and I remained in the car, and he set about his examination in his peculiarly swift yet minute way. The carpet, the chairs, the table, the walls, all underwent inspection. He stood by the uncovered window for some time; he turned about the pens and paper on the table; he pored over the sheet in the typewriter on which the words were printed. At the end the only tangible result in my eyes was a collection of three matches, of which two were wooden and one of wax, three cigar stumps, and a little heap of fragments of mud.

His researches were nearing their conclusion when he caught sight of the knob of a drawer which had rolled into a dark corner under the bunk. He fitted this to a drawer of the desk. The finding of it evidently made him reconstruct his theories, for he went over the carpet once more, pausing a long time under the unshuttered window. Then he turned to the body and lastly fixed his attention on the bed. Behind the pillow lay a book called "Periwinkle," face downward.

"Read himself to sleep," said Joe. "Not much despair about that."

I nodded and made an inquiry.

"A carpet's mighty poor for tracking. Now, if this had happened in the woods, why, I'd be able to say more than that he—"

The conductor pushed open the door and stepped in hurriedly.

"Say, Joe, the evidence is getting to be the sure thing," he exclaimed.

Joe's grey eyes dwelt on the other's excited face for a moment. "Against—"

"Knowles. Who else? He was seen creeping through the sleeping-car after midnight."

"Who saw him?"

"Thompson, the chap with the red head—next berth to this door. He saw Knowles slip by, but didn't think anything of it then."

"Let's talk to Knowles," said Joe.

We were soon face to face with the suspected man. Mrs. Buckman's description, "sour looking and shabby," fitted him very well. He appeared to be about fifty, with stooped but powerful shoulders, and he showed grey about the temples and in his stubble of beard. In the daylight he looked more than shabby, his whole person was unkempt and neglected. At first sight I mistrusted him, and every moment I spent in his company I liked him and his shifty, vindictive face worse. At the first it seemed he would not speak to any purpose, but at length Joe's *bonhomie* and tobacco thawed his reserve.

There were four of us in the uncomfortable privacy of the cook's galley.

"Yes," said Knowles, "it's true I was manager of the Treville depot of the Giant Oil three months ago, and that Buckman got me fired on some liar's evidence. I saw him last evening, and I told him what I thought of him."

"To be exact, you said: 'Look out for yourself?'" interposed Steve, the conductor.

"You were eavesdropping, were you?" Knowles said, looking a little startled. "I may have said something of that sort."

"But what about the second time you saw Buckman?" went on Steve.

"I did not see him a second time."

Here Joe spoke. "The truth is your best card," said he quietly.

Knowles glared like a trapped animal. "Why are you asking me all these questions?" he cried.

"Because Buckman was murdered, choked to death in the small hours of this morning."

Knowles gasped at the words. "Heavens! Is that true?"

"I guess it's no news to you!" snapped out Steve.

"What do you mean by that?"

"We know you passed along through the sleeper just before he was killed. You were seen. We can prove it."

Knowles had gone dead white. "I swear I never saw Buckman but once last night."

"Then what were you doing in the sleeper?"

Joe had stood silent during Steve's questioning, and at this Knowles turned to him.

"I'll tell you just the cold truth," he said. "I did go along. I was mad against Buckman, and I meant to see him and make another appeal."

"Then why didn't you see him?"

"Because I couldn't. I tried, but the door of his car was locked."

"Locked?" cried Joe.

"Shut it, you dead-beat!" sneered Steve. "That yarn won't carry you, for I can prove it's a lie. The door weren't locked when I went along and *found* him dead. You won't tell me he got down to turn the key and then hung himself up again?"

"I'm speaking the truth," reiterated Knowles, "though you are all against me."

Then Joe astonished us.

"I'm not ag'in' you," said he. "I know as well as you do yourself that you did not murder Buckman."

"Bah! Then who did it?" cried the conductor.

"The man who locked the door and who was *inside* when Knowles went along."

Steve thrust out his lip. "Is that so? Well, until he's in handcuffs I'll make sure that Knowles here don't escape."

"All right," said Joe. "Say, Mr. Knowles, let me have a match."

Knowles pulled a box from his pocket.

"Now lay your hand flat on the table," went on Joe.

The large hand, with its grimed and jagged nails, was placed palm downwards for our inspection.

"Look at the thumbs," said Joe.

There was no more said until we were again alone with Steve.

"I'll undertake to smash any case you get up against Knowles, Steve, so as a jury of cottontail rabbits wouldn't convict him," said November.

"I'd like to see you do it!"

"Listen, then. There was two kinds of matches on the floor in the car—here they are." Joe spread them on his palm. "And here's one out of Knowles's box. This wax match was used by Buckman himself, these two wooden ones by the murderer. They're neither of them Knowles's brand, that's plain enough."

"That fact won't carry a jury."

"Not alone," said Joe. "But the next one will. You saw the sharp, broken nails on Knowles's hand. The thumbs had 'em nigh a quarter of an inch long. It's impossible to choke a man to death with nails that length and not tear and scratch the skin of the throat, and you saw for yourself that there isn't a mark on Buckman's throat but bruises only. That's a proof would go with any jury."

The conductor looked a little sheepish. "I'll give you best, Joe. But if it wasn't Knowles, who in creation was it?"

"It was a man twenty years younger than Knowles, very active and strong. A superior chap, trims his nails with scissors, and is, at any rate, fairly educated. He is well acquainted with this line of railway. He boarded the car by the rear door when Buckman and his wife was asleep at some spot where the speed slows down. He was after the report on the Tiger Lily Oilfield. He was searching for it when Buckman woke and jumped at him."

"Why in thunder didn't Buckman give the alarm?"

"Because he tried to get to the bureau without the other seeing."

"To the bureau? What for?"

"For his revolver. He left it in the drawer. And he near got it, too. In the struggle the knob was tore off the drawer."

"But there wasn't a revolver in that drawer. I had a look in it myself!"

"That's so; but it was there till the murderer took it out."

"What did he want it for if he'd got Buckman dead already?"

"A man don't likely hang himself if he's got a revolver handy that'll do the business more comfortably. The finding o' that revolver would, maybe, have spoiled the notion of suicide."

Steve nodded, and Joe continued:—

"Buckman put up a good fight, but the other was too strong for him. That fellow didn't mean to kill Buckman,—I think I can prove that later,—but he had to choke him to prevent his shouting. And when he found he'd done it too hard, like as not he had a bad five minutes. But he was full of cunning, and he hung him up as a blind. Then he locked the door and sat there in Buckman's chair and smoked one of Buckman's cigars."

"What?" exclaimed Steve. "With Buckman hanging there?"

"Sure! There was three cigar stumps. Two of them Buckman had smoked through a holder, but the end of the third was all chewed. I tell you the murderer sat there and smoked and thought out what he'd do, for Buckman's death was awkward in two or three ways. He sat there for nigh on twenty minutes, and now and again he'd go to the window that he'd slipped the shutter from and look out."

"Tracked him on the carpet?" inquired Steve, who was still a bit sore on the matter of Knowles.

Joe grinned significantly. "Yes, and found he had wet mud on his moccasins. That's how I first made sure it wasn't you, Steve. Your soles were dry when I looked at them, and you have boots to your feet, anyway."

Steve's ejaculation cannot be set down here.

"He kep' going to the window," continued Joe, "'cos he wanted to locate the spot where he reckoned he'd slip off the car. I told you he knew the line well. Say, Steve, ain't there any curve where the engine slows down that you pass about one o'clock?"

"She slows down just before she gets to the big trestle bridge over the Shimpanny Lake."

Joe pondered a minute. "He jumped off there, and that means he had a bit of time to think out what he'd do. You see, his plan hadn't worked out according to rule—to my way of thinking."

"How so?"

"I'll tell you all that later."

"You're a fair terror, Joe. You ought to have that chap in a net. Where did he board us, anyway?"

"Don't know. But it wasn't long afore he killed Buckman, 'cos his moccasins hadn't had time to dry. And that proves, too, that he wasn't hid on the cars since the last stop. Now what we've got to think about is catching him. I suppose I can get a fast engine at Seven Springs and go back down the line?"

"Sure," said Steve.

Twenty minutes later we arrived at Seven Springs, and in less than twenty minutes more November Joe and I, with a representative of the Provincial Police, were steaming back along the line. And we travelled at a speed which I believe was the greatest ever attempted over those metals. At length our engine thundered over the Shimpanny Lake and drew up. We descended, and began to search both sides of the line. A call from Joe brought us running to him.

"Here's where he jumped," he said. "See! He lost his footing and rolled down the bank."

At the spot where we were standing the railway line passed along the top of a high embankment, the south side of which was grown with a sprinkling of wild raspberry bushes. Beside the permanent way there were the deep prints of two moccasined feet; from them to the bottom of the bank a path had been ploughed through the broken canes to the foot of some spruces.

"He pitched down here like a sack," said Joe. "The train must have been going pretty fast—faster than he counted for. See here ag'in, the spruces. He got to his feet. Come on, there's his trail."

We followed it without difficulty for about fifty yards, and then we came upon a sapling spruce freshly cut down, about a foot above the ground; the head of it, with the little branches and leaves, lay scattered about.

Joe and the police trooper, whose name was Polloks, examined the little tree with its jagged cuts very carefully, November even lifting the chips of wood and bark which were spread about on the ground.

"What was he up to here, I wonder?" said Polloks. "He hasn't made a fire."

"No," said Joe shortly, and hurried away upon the trail.

For another hundred yards the tracks were plain among the raspberry canes, then they climbed the embankment, and finally disappeared altogether.

Polloks swore. "He's done us here!" he cried. "He walked along the metals; no one can tell which way he's gone."

"Huh! He won't get shut of us," said November Joe, "not that way. Where's the nearest post-office on the line?"

"At Silent Water."

"You go and call up the engine, Polloks. It's Silent Water for us as fast as we can get there."

Polloks wasted no time, and once more we were flying along the line.

"The express passed Shimpanny Trestle at three-twenty this morning," shouted the trooper through the din of our travelling, "and it's seven now. Our man's got near four hours' start if he's ahead of us, but it's eighteen miles to Silent Water, so we may just nip him on the permanent way."

But, with the keenest lookout, we came in sight of no figure ahead of us before we reached Silent Water. It is a very small township, and we slipped through the depot so as to arouse no curiosity, and only stopped the engine a couple of hundred yards beyond to give us time to jump off. We hurried back to the post-office.

"Any fellow with his right arm in a sling been posting a letter here?" inquired Joe of the postmaster.

"None."

"Sure?"

"Been here all morning."

Joe pulled Polloks aside. "Quick! Work the telephone and have every post-office within twenty miles around watched. If a man with his right arm in a sling comes along to post a letter, arrest him. He'll be wearing cowhide moccasins, and a good size. But it was here I expected he'd aim for."

Polloks had hardly got to the telephone when Joe swung round, and, catching him by the shoulder, forced him down behind the counter out of sight. The next moment a tall young man with his arm in a rough sling opened the door of the post-office.

"Two-cent stamp," he said curtly to the postmaster.

The stamp was handed out, and as the stranger turned to go he held it between his lips, plunging his left hand into his pocket. I saw him pull out a long envelope, and at that instant Joe and Polloks leapt upon him.

"What in—" yelled the man.

But November Joe had seized the letter.

"Hold your man, Polloks. Look, this letter is addressed to the Giant Oilfields Head Offices. It is the Tiger Lily Report, and that is the murderer of Fletcher Buckman."

"It was sure easy," said Joe as we travelled up the line again, "from the moment I saw the mud stains on the carpet in Buckman's car. They were still wet, and when the murder was done we'd been going without a stop for three hours—time for any boots to dry in them heated cars. So it wasn't any one on the train—that was clear.

"Then whoever done it must 'a' been young and active, or he could never board a train travelling at fifteen mile an hour, and he must have been fairly educated or he couldn't have used the type-writer. Again, he must have been well acquainted with the railway."

"How could you tell that?"

"You remember that the blind was up off one window in Buckman's car. Again and again the murderer went to that window—I could tell by the tracks on the carpet. Now, why did he do that, unless he was looking for the place where he meant to jump off, and how could he recognize that place unless he knew the line?"

I thought I detected a flaw in November Joe's reasoning.

"Perhaps he was just waiting for the train to slow down," I said.

"No," replied Joe. "If he had been he'd never have lighted that cigar. The fact of his lighting that proves that he must 'a' known that he had twenty minutes to wait; and it proves that he was a mighty cool hand, too!"

I nodded.

"As for Knowles," continued Joe, "why, you heard more'n one reason why he was plumb out of it. The cigar and the matches and the wild-cat nails he carried."

"But how could you guess this fellow had his arm in a sling?"

"You mind that cut sapling near where he tumbled off the cars? He hadn't took away two foot of it. What did he want a bit of spruce that length for? It wouldn't be to help him walk, or I'd 'a' guessed a sprained ankle. I fancied it might be for a splint. He wouldn't fall soft off the cars, you bet."

"But you said it was his right arm?"

"Look at the way he hacked the spruce! The clumsy way a man would with his left hand. That meant he'd damaged his right."

"But how did you know he'd want to post that letter, and post it at Silent Water? Why, it would have seemed more likely he'd make away across country."

"The post-office at Silent Water was a dead cert. I'll explain that, but you must go back a bit. You see, that chap only meant to get a forward look-in at the report; his game and the game of the people he was working for was to forestall the rest of the world in knowing what Buckman's decision was. He did not want to kill Buckman, only matters turned that way. Then he had to take away the report, for it wasn't a cent o' use to him until it was in the hands of the Giant Oil Company, and he had to get it there without any notion of its having been tampered with. His idea was to go back along the line and post it just where Buckman might have posted it himself. He trusted to the suicide dodge to hold up suspicion till he was through with his plan."

"But would the Giant Oil Company act on the report after hearing of Buckman's horrible death?" I argued.

"Why not?" said Joe. "All they'd think was he'd had it posted the night before, just as soon as he'd finished writing it. Yes, they'd 'a' acted on it, and this chap—I haven't got his name yet—would 'a' cleaned up a good many hundred thousand dollars!"

"By the way, Joe," I said. "Where is Buckman's report?"

Joe smiled. "On its way to Giant Oil by this. We mailed it."

"I wonder if it was favourable?"

"We couldn't open it, you know, but the chap had a slip o' paper on him on which he'd written a telegraph message. Just one word— '*Buy.*' So I guess you can buy me fifteen shares in Tiger Lily as soon as you like, Mr. Quaritch," replied November. "I've got the money, for I trapped a silver fox last winter; this report'll maybe turn it into a gold one! You light out and buy some shares, too, and then maybe you'll make that trip to Africa we've so often yarned about. I'd like to shoot one of them lions. I see one once to a fair, near Levis, and you could hear him roaring out on the ferry halfway across to Quebec. I'd sure like to copy 'T. R.,' and down one of they."

11
Linda Petersham

November Joe had bidden me farewell at the little siding known by the picturesque name of Silent Water.

"'Spect you'll be back again, Mr. Quaritch, as soon as you've fixed them new mining contracts, and then, maybe, we'll try a wolf-hunt. There's a tidy pack comes out on the Lac Noir ice when it's moonlight. The forest's wonderful still them frosty nights, a fella can hear a owl miles and miles."

I assured Joe that I would do my best to return, but as a matter of fact, fate was against me all that winter, and it was only now and again that I heard from Joe, who had gone over the Maine border on a trapping expedition. Often and often, as I sat at my roll-topped desk and studied the outlook of eaves smothered in snow and bare telegraph-poles, my mind would switch off to picture November boiling his lunch-kettle in the lee of a boulder, and I would feel irresistibly drawn to close the desk aforesaid and go to join him. I was very sure of my welcome.

But the shackles of business are not so easily shaken off, and the spring had already come before another vacation in the woods had begun to merge into possibility. About this time I paid one of my periodical visits to Boston, and it was while I was there in the office of my agents and correspondents that Linda Petersham rang me up on the telephone and demanded my presence at lunch.

"But I am engaged," said I.

"Then you must put your engagement off."

"I don't see how I can. Will to-morrow—"

"No—to-morrow will do for him—whoever he is. *I* want you to-day."

"What is it?"

"I will tell you when you come. I want you."

I made another effort to explain my position, but Linda had said her last word and rung off. I smiled as I called up the picture of a small Greek head crowned with golden hair, a pair of dark blue eyes and a mouth wearing a rather imperious expression.

The end of it was that I went, for I have known Linda all her life, and the fact that breaking my previous appointment lost me the option of purchase of a valuable mine caused me little trouble, for to be able to pay for one's pleasures is one of the few assets of the very rich, and speaking personally I have all my life seized every opportunity of escape from the tyranny of the millions that I have inherited and accumulated. I have cared little for the pursuit of money—the reason perhaps why everything I have touched has turned to gold.

The Petersham family consists of Linda and her father, and though in business relations Mr. Petersham is a power to be reckoned with, at home he exists for the sole apparent purpose of carrying out his charming daughter's wishes. It is a delightful house to go to, for they are the happiest people I know, and the moment one sets foot inside their doors one's spirits begin to rise. I said as much to Linda as we shook hands.

"That speaks well for my self-command, for I happen to be feeling pretty mean to-day. Come, we'll go in to lunch at once."

I found myself the only guest, which surprised me, for the Petersham mansion has a reputation for hospitality.

"Really, Linda, this is very charming of you. I wonder how much Tom Getchley or that young Van Home would give to be in my place at this moment," I said, as we sat down.

Linda looked at me with far-away eyes.

"What? You mean lunching alone with me?"

"Yes, it is an unexpected pleasure."

"Dear James! it is not a pleasure at all, it is a necessity. I want to talk to you."

"So you said before. Go ahead, then; I'm ready."

"Not now; after lunch."

We carried on a fragmentary conversation while the servants waited on us, and all the time I was wondering what on earth Linda could have to say to me. It was evidently something of the deepest importance in her eyes, for she was obviously absorbed in thinking about it, and answered my remarks at random.

When at last we were together in her boudoir, she began at once.

"James, I want you to do this for me. I want you to persuade Pop not to do something."

"I? I persuade him? You don't need me for that; you, who can make him do or not do anything, just as you wish."

"I thought I could, but I find I can't."

"How is that?"

"Well, he is set on going back to Kalmacks."

"Kalmacks?"

Linda opened her blue eyes upon me.

"Haven't you heard?"

"Heard what?"

"Where in the world were you last September?"

"Camped in the woods of Maine and Beauce."

"That accounts for it. But you have heard of Kalmacks?"

"I know it is the place Julius Fischer built up in the mountains. He used to go shooting and fishing there."

"That is it. It's a place you'd love; lots of good rooms, and standing 'way back on a mountain slope with miles of view and a stream tumbling past the very door. Father bought it last year, and with it all the sporting rights Julius Fischer claimed. The woods are full of moose and there are beaver and otter . . . and that's where the trouble came in."

"But Fischer had trouble from the day he went up to shoot at Kalmacks. He had to run for it, so I was told. Didn't your father know that? Why did Mr. Petersham have anything to do with the place?"

"Oh, it was just one of Pop's notions, I suppose," said Linda, with the rather weary tolerance of the modern daughter.

"They are a dangerous lot round there!"

"He knew that. They are squatters, trappers who have squatted among those woods and hills for generations. Of course they think the country belongs to them. Pop knew that, and in his opinion the compensation Julius Fischer offered and gave them was inadequate."

"It would be!" I commented. I could without effort imagine Julius Fischer's views on compensation, for I had met him in business.

"Well, father went into the matter, and he found that the squatters had a good deal to be said for their side of the case, so that he did what he thought was fair by them."

I nodded. "If I know him, he did more than that!"

"That's nice of you, James. Anyway, he paid them good high prices for their rights, or what they considered to be their rights, for in law, of course, they possessed none. Every one seemed pleased and satisfied, and we were looking forward to going there this spring for the fishing, when news came that one of father's game-wardens had been shot at."

"Shot at?"

Linda nodded the Greek head I admired so much.

"Yes. Last autumn father put on a couple of wardens to look after the game, and they have been there all winter. From their reports they have got on quite well with the squatters, and now suddenly, for no reason that they can guess, one of them, William Worke by name, has been fired upon in his camp."

"Killed?" I asked.

"No, but badly wounded. He said he was sure the bullet could have been put into his heart just as easily, but it was sent through his knee, by way of a notice to quit he thinks."

"Those folks up there must be half savages."

"They are, but that's not all. Three days ago a letter came, meant for father, but addressed to me. Whoever wrote it must have seen father and knew that he was not the kind of man who could be readily frightened, so they thought they would get at him through me. It was a horrible letter."

"Can I see it?"

Linda unlocked a drawer and handed me a piece of soiled paper. The words were written upon a sheet torn from an old account-book. They ran as follows:—

> You, Petersham, you mean skunk! Don't you come in our wods unles yor willing to pay five thousand dollars. Bring the goods and youl be told wher to put it, so it will come into the hands of riters. Dollars ain't nothin to you, but they can keep an expanding bulet out yor hide.

"What do you think of that?" asked Linda.

"It may be a hoax."

"Now, James, what is the good of saying such a silly thing to me? Father pretends to think the same. But, of course, I know these men mean business. And equally, of course, you agree with me?"

I hesitated.

"Do you think it *is* a hoax?"

"Well, no, I can't honestly say I do."

"Which means, in plain language, that if father does not pay up that five thousand dollars, he will be shot."

"Not necessarily. He need not go up to Kalmacks this fall."

"But of course he will go! He's more set on going than ever. You know father when he's dealing with men. And he persists in his opinion that the letter is probably only bluff."

"Does he guess who wrote it?"

"No, he has no idea at all."

I considered for a little before I spoke. "Linda, have you really sent for me to try to persuade your father that it would be wiser for him not to go to Kalmacks?"

Linda's lip curled scornfully. "I should not put it just like that! I can imagine father's answer if you did! . . . I'm afraid it will be no good letting you say anything, you don't know how."

"You mean that I have no tact?"

She smiled at me, and I instantly forgave her. "Well, perhaps I do, but you know it is far better to be able to give help than just to talk about it."

"I am ready to help you in any possible way."

"Of course! I relied on that."

"But how *can* I help?"

"I will tell you. Father is determined on going to Kalmacks, and I want you to come with us."

"Us?" I cried.

"Naturally I'm going."

"But it is absurd! Your father would never allow it!"

"He can't prevent it, dear James," she said softly. "Besides, what is there against my going?"

"The danger."

She thrust out her round resolute chin. "I don't for a moment suppose that even the Kalmacks people would attack a woman. And father is all that I have in the world. I'm going."

"Then I suppose I shall have to go too. But tell me what purpose does your father think he will serve by undertaking this very risky expedition?"

"He believes that the general feeling up at Kalmacks is in his favour, and that the shooting of the warden as well as the writing of this letter is the work of a small band of individuals who wish to blackmail him. We will be quite a strong party, and he hopes to discover who is threatening him. By the way, didn't I hear from Sir Andrew McLerrick that you had been in the woods all these last falls with a wonderful guide who could read trails like Uncas, the last of the Delawares, or one of those old trappers one reads of in Fenimore Cooper's novels?"

"That's true."

"What is his name?"

"November Joe."

"November Joe," she repeated. "I visualize him at once. A wintry-looking old man, with a grey goatee and piercing eyes."

I burst out laughing. "It's extraordinary you should hit him off so well."

"He must come too," she commanded.

"He is probably a hundred miles deep in the Maine woods."

"Then you must fetch him out. That's all!"

"If I can reach him, I will. Give me two cable forms; there is no time to lose."

Linda found me what I required, and bent over my shoulder while I wrote. I cabled to Joe:—

> Come to Quebec immediately, prepared for month's camping trip. Most important.
> Quaritch.

That was my first cable. My second was addressed to Mrs. Harding, at Harding's Farm, Beauce, the little post-office where November periodically called for his letters. It ran:—

> Am sending cable to November Joe. Hustle special messenger with it to middle of Maine if necessary. Will pay.
> James Quaritch.

Linda read them both. "Why *Mrs*. Harding?" she asked.

"Because one capable woman is worth ten ordinary men."

Linda looked at me thoughtfully.

"I do occasionally realize why you've been so successful in business, James. In spite of appearance you are really quite a capable person. And," she added impulsively, "you are also a dear, and I am immensely grateful."

Soon after I took my leave. The next day I received this reply from Joe.

> Expect me dawn, Friday.
> November.

I rang up Linda and read out the message. "Good Old Mossback!" said she.

12
KALMACKS

On Friday I got Joe—who, true to his promise, had, I heard, arrived at dawn in Quebec—on the long-distance telephone, and by that means arranged that he should meet us at Priamville, the nearest point on the railway to those mountains in the heart of which the estate of Kalmacks was situated. I myself arranged to accompany the Petershams.

Into the story of our journey to Priamville I need not go, but will pick up the sequence of events at the moment of our arrival at that enterprising town, when Linda, looking from the car window, suddenly exclaimed:—

"Look at that *magnificent* young man!"

"Which one?" I asked innocently, as I caught sight of November's tall figure awaiting us.

"How many men in sight answer my description?" she retorted. "Of course I mean the woodsman. Why, he's coming this way. I must speak to him."

Before I could answer, she had jumped lightly to the platform, and turning to Joe with a childlike expression in her blue eyes, said:—

"Oh, can you tell me how many minutes this train stops here?"

"It don't generally stop here at all, but they flagged her because they're expecting passengers. Can I help you any, miss?"

"It's very kind of you."

At this moment I appeared from the car. "Hullo, Joe!" said I. "How are things?"

"All right, Mr. Quaritch. There's two slick buckboards with a pair of horses to each waiting, and a wagonette fit for the King o' Russia. The road between this and the mountains is flooded by beaver working in a backwater 'bout ten mile out. They say we can drive through all right. Miss Petersham needn't fear getting too wet."

"How do you know my name?" exclaimed Linda.

"I heard you described, miss," replied Joe gravely.

Linda looked at me.

"Good for the Old Mossback!" said I.

Her lips bent into a sudden smile. "You must be Mr. November Joe. I have heard so much of you from Mr. Quaritch. You were in the Maine woods when you got his cable, weren't you?"

"Yes. Mrs. Harding sent it along by an Indian. He near missed me, but I come on his tracks following my line of traps. I guessed from them he had a message for me."

Linda opened her eyes. "You guessed from his tracks that he had a message for you! I don't understand."

"It's plumb simple," said Joe. "He kept cutting for my trail all along the line of traps, but never visited none of them. An Indian won't never pass down a line of traps without having a look to see what's caught; he's that curious unless he's in a hurry and got some object. And why should this Indian come chasin' after me so fast unless he had a message for me? But I'm talking, and anyways, I got the message. Give me them bags, Mr. Quaritch."

We went out, and loaded our baggage upon the waiting buckboards. One of these was driven by a small, sallow-faced man, who turned out to be the second game-warden, Puttick.

Mr. Petersham asked how Bill Worke, the wounded man, was progressing.

"He's coming along pretty tidy, Mr. Petersham, but he'll carry a stiff leg with him all his life."

"I'm sorry for that. I suppose you have found out nothing further as to the identity of the man who fired the shot?"

"Nothing," said Puttick, "and not likely to. They're all banded together up there."

On which cheerful information our little caravan started. At Linda's wish Joe took the place of the driver of Mr. Petersham's light imported wagonette, and as we went along, she gave him a very clear story of the sequence of events, to all of which he listened with the characteristic series of "Well, nows!" and "You don't says!" with which he was in the habit of punctuating the remarks of a lady. He said them, as usual, in a voice which not only emphasized the facts at exactly the right places, but also lent an air of subtle compliment to the eloquence of the narrator.

And so we went onwards. At first over flat expanses of muddy plain, splashing axle-high through the mire of the so-called road, until at last the purple mountains ahead of us began to turn blue, hardening again to green as we neared the foothills. And all the time I found myself envying November Joe.

When we stopped near a patch of pine trees to partake of an impromptu lunch, it was his quick hands that prepared the camp-fire, and his skilled axe that fashioned the rude but comfortable seats. It was he also who disappeared for a moment to return with three half-pound trout, that he had taken by some swift process of his own from the brook of which we only heard the murmur. And for all these doings he received an amount of open admiration from Linda's blue eyes, which seemed to me almost exaggerated.

"I think your November Joe is a perfect dear," she confided to me.

"If you really think that," said I, "have mercy on him! You do not want to add his scalp to all the others."

"Many of the others are bald," said she. "His hair would furnish a dozen of them!"

So the afternoon passed away, and as it became late, we entered great tracks of gloomy pine woods. A wind, which had risen with the evening, moaned through their tops, and flung the dark waters of innumerable little lakes against their moss-bordered shores.

I noticed that Puttick unslung his rifle and laid it among the packs upon the buckboard beside him, and whenever the road dipped to a more than usually sombre defile, his eyes, quick and restless as those of some forest animal, darted and peered into the shadows. The light of the sun was fading when there occurred the one incident of our journey. It was not of real importance, but I think it made an impression on all of us. The road along which we were driving came suddenly out into an open space, and here in front of a shack of the roughest description a man was engaged in cutting logs. As we passed, he glanced up at us, and his face was like that of some mediaeval prisoner—a tangle of wild beard, a mass of greyish hair, and among it all a pair of eyes which seemed to glare forth hatred. It may have been, indeed, it probably was, merely the rooted and natural dislike of strangers, so common to the mountain districts, but to us, wrought up with the stories we had heard, there was something ominous about the wolfish face.

It was already dark when we arrived at the house, a long, low building of surprising spaciousness, set literally among the pines, the fragrant branches of which tapped and rustled upon the windows. In the midst of a peaceful countryside it would be hard to imagine a more delightful summer residence, but here, in this wild district, the gloom of the thick woods that surrounded us on all sides was daunting.

We went in, and while dinner was preparing, Mr. Petersham, Joe, and I went to the room where the wounded game-warden, Worke, lay upon a bed smoking a pipe with a candle guttering on a chair beside him.

"Yes, Mr. Petersham," said he, in answer to a question. "When you went away last fall I did think things was settling down a bit; and, indeed, all was quiet enough through the winter. I'm not saying that there wasn't some trapping done, but it was most all over the lands where you gave liberty. The squatters, wild as they are, seemed contented-like, and though they wasn't friends with us game-wardens,—which couldn't be expected,—they wasn't enemies either. Well, Friday, a week ago, while Puttick was on the eastern boundary, I thought I'd go up to Senlis Lake, where last year Keoghan had the brook netted. I went along, but I was a bit late starting, so that it was dusk before I got my camp tidied up to rights. I was making a fire to boil my kettle, when a shot was fired from the rocks up above, and the next I knew was that I was hit pretty bad through this knee."

"From how far away was the shot fired?"

"Eighty yards, or maybe a hundred."

"Go on."

"As I say, it was coming on dark, and I rolled into a bush for cover, but whoever it were didn't fire at me again. I don't think he wanted to kill me, if he had he could have put the bullet into my heart just as easy as in my leg. I tied up the wound the best way I could, lucky the bullet hadn't touched any big artery. Next morning I crawled up the hill and lit signal smokes, till Puttick came. He brought me in here."

"I suppose Puttick had a look round for the tracks of the fella who gunned you?" asked November.

"He did, but he didn't find out nothing. There was a light shower between dark and dawn, and the ground on the hill above there is mostly rock."

"Well, Bill," said Mr. Petersham, "I'm sorry you got wounded this way in my employ. I suppose you have not the slightest suspicion as to who it was fired at you."

Worke shook his head. "Nary notion," said he.

13
THE MEN OF THE MOUNTAINS

Such, then, was the story of our coming to Kalmacks, and for the next two or three days we spent our time fishing in the streams, the only move in the direction of the main object of our visit being that Joe, whom Linda insisted upon accompanying, walked over to Senlis Lake and had a look at the scene of Worke's accident. The old tracks, of course, were long since washed away, and I thought with the others that Joe's visit had been fruitless, until he showed me the shell of an exploded cartridge.

"The bullet which went through Bill Worke's leg came out of that. I found it on the hill above. It's a 45-75 central fire Winchester, the old '76 model."

"This is a great discovery you and Miss Petersham have made."

"She don't know nothing about it," said November. "It's best she shouldn't, Mr. Quaritch."

"Do you mean to say you found this and never told her?"

Joe smiled. "There's nothing much to it, anyway; she lost her brooch somewhere by the lake, and was lookin' for it when I found this." Joe indicated the exploded shell. "The mountains is full of 45-75 Winchesters, 1876 pattern. Some years back a big ironmongery store down here went bust and threw a fine stock of them calibre rifles on the market. A few dollars would buy one, so there's one in pretty nigh every house, and two and three in some. Howsoever, it may be useful to know that him that shot Bill Worke carried that kind o' a rifle; still, we'd best keep it to ourselves, Mr. Quaritch."

169

"All right," said I. "By the way, Joe, there's a side to the situation I don't understand. We've been here four days and nothing has happened. I mean Mr. Petersham has had no word of where to put the five thousand dollars blackmail these criminals are demanding of him."

"Maybe there's a reason for that."

"I can't think of any."

"What about the sand?"

"The sand?" I repeated.

"Yes, haven't you noticed? I got Mr. Petersham to have two loads of sand brought up from the lake, and laid all round the house. It takes a track wonderful. I guess it's pretty near impossible to come nigh the house without leaving a clear trail. But the first rainy night, I mean when there's rain enough to wash out tracks . . ."

"They'll come?"

"Yes, they'll likely come."

But as it happened Joe was wrong. I believe that his reasoning was correct enough, and that it was the fear of leaving such marks as would enable us to gather something of their identity that kept the enemy from pinning upon our door the letter which finally arrived prosaically enough in a cheap store envelope that bore the Priamville postmark. The contents of this letter were as follows:—

> Petersham, you go alone to Butler's Cairn II
> o'clock Friday night. Take the dollars along; youl be
> met their and can hand it over.

Below was a rude drawing of a coffin.

Petersham read the note out to Joe and myself.

"Where's Butler's Cairn?" he asked.

"I know it," said November. "Butler's Cairn is on a hill about two miles west of here."

"I suppose you won't go?" said I.

"With the money? Certainly not!"

"You can hardly go without it."

"Why not?"

"You would be shot down."

"I'd talk to the ruffians first, and then if there was any shooting, I guess I'd be as much in it as they would."

"I suggest that we all three go," I said.

But Joe would have none of this plan.

"There's nothing to be gained by that, Mr. Quaritch. You bet these fellas'll keep a pretty bright lookout. If they saw three of us coming, they'd shoot as like as not."

"We can shoot also, I suppose!"

"That's true, Mr. Petersham, but it ain't likely we'd *hit* any one. These chaps'll hide in among the rocks. They'd see us plain, for there is a bit of a moon, but we wouldn't get an eye on them. No, we can't do no good that-a-ways," said Joe.

"How can we do any good, as you call it, at all?"

"I was thinking I might slip right along to Butler's Cairn and maybe get a look at the fellas."

"No!" said Petersham, decidedly. "I won't allow it. You say yourself you would be shot."

"I said *we* would get shot, not me alone. Three men can't go quiet where one can."

"You think they will be at Butler's Cairn whether I go there or not?"

"Sure. They want to know if you're giving in, and they won't be able to tell unless they go and see. Now, Mr. Quaritch, you tell Mr. Petersham there ain't much danger for me, seeing I've learnt to move quiet in the woods. I'll try my luck to-night."

And so finally it was arranged, though not without a good deal of argument with Petersham.

The evening fell wild and windy, but with a clear sky save for occasional fleecy clouds that raced across the face of the moon. Joe took advantage of one of these dark intervals to drop out of one of the back windows, and was immediately swallowed up into the night.

"That's a fine fellow," remarked Petersham.

I nodded.

"The kind of fellow who fought with and bettered the Iroquois at their own game. I wonder what he will see at Butler's Cairn."

It was past midnight when Joe appeared again. Petersham and I both asked for his news.

November shook his head. "I've nothing to tell; nothing at all. I didn't see no one."

"What? You mean that no one came after all?" exclaimed Petersham.

"Not that I saw."

"Where were you?"

"Lying down on top of the Cairn itself. There's good corners to it."

"You could see well round, then, and if any one had come you would not have failed to observe them."

"Couldn't be too sure. There was some dark times when the moon was shut in by clouds. They might 'a' come them times, though I don't think they did. But I'll know for certain soon, unless it comes on heavy rain. . . . There's a fine little lake they calls Butler's Pond up there. You take your fish-pole, Mr. Quaritch, and we'll go over at sunrise and you try for some of them trout, while I take a scout round for tracks."

This we did, but search as Joe would, he failed to discover any sign at all. He told me this when he joined me at breakfast-time.

"Evidently no one came," I said, as I watched him fry the bacon over a small fire.

"That's so."

After I had caught a nice string of trout, we walked back to Kalmacks, circling round the house before we entered it. The sand lay undisturbed by any strange footstep, but when we got in we found Mr. Petersham in a state of the greatest excitement.

"One of the blackmailers has had a long talk with Puttick!" he told us.

"What?"

"Incredible as it sounds, it is so."

"But when was this?"

"Early this morning, some time after you and Joe started. This is how it happened. Puttick had just got up and gone down with a tin of rosin and some spare canvas and tin to mend that canoe we

ripped on the rock yesterday. In fact he had only just begun working, when he was startled by a voice ordering him to hold up his
hands."

"By Jove! What next?"

"Why, he held them up. He had no choice. And then a man
stepped out from behind the big rock that's just above where the
canoe lies."

"I hope Puttick recognized him?"

"No; the fellow had a red handkerchief tied over his nose and
mouth, only his eyes showed under the brim of a felt hat that was
pulled low down over them. He carried a rifle that he kept full on
Puttick's chest while they talked. . . . But I'll call Puttick, he can
finish the account of the affair himself. That's best."

Puttick answered to the call, and after running over the story
which was exactly similar to that we had just heard from Petersham, he continued:—

"The tough had a red hanker tied over his ugly face, nothing
but his eyes showing. He had me covered with his gun to rights all
the time."

"What kind of a gun was it?"

"I didn't see; leastways, I didn't notice."

"Well, had he anything to say?"

"He kep' me that way a minute before he started speaking. 'You
tell Petersham,' says he, 'it's up to him to pay right away. Tell him
unless he goes at once to Butler's Cairn and takes the goods and
leaves them there on the big flat stone by the rock, he'll hear from
us afore evening, and he'll hear in a way that'll make him sorry all
his life. And as for you, Ben Puttick, you take a hint and advise old
man Petersham to buy us off, and he can't be too quick about doing it either. If he tries escape we'll get him on the road down to
Priamville.' After he'd done talking, he made me put my watch on
the canoe—that I'd turned bottom up to get at that rent—and
warned me not to move for half an hour. When the half-hour was
up, I come right away and tell you."

"How was the chap dressed?" inquired Joe.

"Like most of 'em. Dark old coat and ragged pair of trousers
and moccasins."

"What colour was his socks?"

"Couldn't see. He had his trousers stuffed into them kind o'
half-boot moccasins that buckle at the knee. The stores to
Priamville are full of them."

"Tailor short was he?"

"Medium-like."

"Which way did he go when he left you?"

"West; right along the bank."

"You followed his trail after the half-hour was over?"

Puttick opened his eyes. "He didn't leave none."

"Left no trail! How's that?" cried Petersham.

But Joe interposed. "You mean he kep' to the stones in the bed
o' the brook all the time?"

"That's it. And, anyway, if I'd got fooling lookin' for his tracks
I'd 'a' got a bullet in me same as Bill Worke," ended the little man.
"They're all watching for us."

We were silent for a moment. Then Petersham turned to
Puttick.

"What do you think of it, Ben? You have some experience of
these squatters up here. Do you think they mean business?"

"There ain't much fooling about these mountain men," Puttick
answered bitterly. "And now I says this to you, Mr. Petersham, and
I can't never say nothing stronger. If you're minded to stay on here
at this place, you must pay."

"You know well enough I don't intend to pay."

"Listen a bit, Mr. Petersham. Here's my notion. You'd best pay
if you don't want . . ." the warden paused.

"What? What? Go on!"

"If you don't want Miss Petersham hurt or killed."

"My daughter?"

"That's how I read it. What else could he mean? He said you'd
be sorry all your life."

"Good Heavens! Even the most hardened ruffians would not
hurt a woman. You don't think it possible?" Petersham turned to me.

"I think that Linda runs a very great risk by staying."

"Then she shall go."

But when Linda was called and the facts made clear to her, she absolutely refused to leave Kalmacks.

"You will force me to pay the money then," said Petersham, "though I am well aware that this demand will only be the first of many. Whenever these blackmailers want a thousand dollars, aye, or ten thousand dollars, they know they will only have to ask me to supply them. But I can't risk you—I'll pay."

Joe turned to Petersham. "If you climb down now, I'll be right sorry I ever come with you. I don't hold with backing down under a bluff."

I, who knew Joe, was surprised to hear him offer so definite an opinion in such strong terms, but Linda clapped her hands.

"It's all nonsense, isn't it? Why, if any one attempted to hurt me, Joe would make him regret it; wouldn't you, Joe?" She flashed him a glance of her glorious eyes.

"I'd sure try to hard enough," replied November. "And now, Mr. Quaritch, I'll ask Ben here to show me just where the fella stood when he held him up this morning."

So Joe went down to the brook, and I went with him. We were soon beside the canoe which Puttick had been mending.

"Here's where I was, and there's where he stood," said Puttick, pointing to a small mass of rock close by. "And there's the place I set down my watch."

November glanced over the details and then followed the bank of the brook for some distance. Presently he returned.

"Did you strike his trail?" asked Puttick.

"No, the stones lead right away to the lake, and like as not he came in a canoe."

"Like as not," agreed Puttick, and resumed his work on the canoe which had been so rudely interrupted earlier in the day.

We found Linda in the living-room arranging some fishing-tackle. She at once appealed to Joe.

"Oh, Joe, I want to try some of those English lures Mr. Quaritch gave me. I'm going to fish and I want to use this two-jointed pole; will you fix it for me?"

Joe took the rod and, as he examined it, said:—

"I'd like you to make me a promise, Miss Linda."

"What is it?"

"Not to go out at all to-day."

"But, Joe, it's such a lovely day and you know you thought all that man's talk with Ben Puttick was bluff; that there is really not any danger."

"I didn't say that, Miss Linda."

Linda looked at him in surprise. "But you advised father not to send me away!"

"I know." Joe smiled. "And Mr. Petersham is that angry, he won't speak to me."

"You don't think I'm in danger?'"

"You're in great danger, Miss Linda."

"From whom?"

"It's hard to say."

"But I can't stay indoors indefinitely. And anyway, I don't be-lieve they would attack a woman, though if they did you would catch them, Joe."

"I dunno—and it wouldn't be much good after they'd hurt you—perhaps hurt you bad."

"Then you must go out with me, Joe. If you are with me, they will not dare . . ."

Joe had fixed the fishing-rod by this time. He handed it back to Linda.

"Look here, Miss Linda, if you'll stay in the house just over to-day, I wouldn't wonder but it might be quite safe for you to go out tomorrow—and ever after."

"Joe! You mean you have discovered—"

"No; I ain't discovered nothing, but if you stay in the way I ask, maybe I shall." Joe took up his hat.

"Where are you going, November?" I asked.

"Over to Senlis Lake, Mr. Quaritch. Will you see Ben Puttick and tell him I won't be back till lateish and will he cook the pota-toes and the corn-flour cakes, if I don't get back to time? Miss Linda, will you please tell every one, even your father, that you have a mighty painful head and that's why you're staying in?"

"Yes, Joe," said Linda.'

14

THE MAN IN THE BLACK HAT

After Joe's departure I took my rod and went down to the brook where I fished throughout the morning. The rise, however, was poor, so I returned to the house, and after lunch I took a book and sat with it in the verandah, where I was joined in due course by Linda and Mr. Petersham.

"It's cool here; the only cool spot in the place to-day," remarked Petersham.

"Yes, and don't the spruces smell sweet?" said Linda. "Joe cut them to give me shade."

She pointed to a row of tall saplings propped against the rail of the verandah, so as to form a close screen.

"Joe always thinks of things for people," she added.

Petersham glanced from me to Linda. "If your headache is bad, you had better lie down in the house," he said.

"It is ever so much better, but I'll fetch some smelling-salts."

I was about to offer to bring them for her when I caught her father's eye behind her back and remained where I was. As soon as she had gone in, Petersham stepped up to me and whispered:—

"To give her shade!" he repeated.

I looked round and nodded.

"There is always shade here," he went on. "The sun can't get in through the pines on this side; the wood is thickest here."

"That's true," I agreed, looking at the close-grown junipers that stood in front of us. "Joe stacked these saplings against the rail for some other reason."

"Of course! He knew that Linda would very likely sit here, and he was afraid."

"Afraid? Of what?" said Linda suddenly, from behind us. "No one could hurt me here. Why, I could call for help and you are both here; you could protect me."

"Not against a rifle-bullet," said Petersham. "For my sake, go in, Linda!"

As he said the words from far away came the sound of a shot. Distance robbed it of that acrimony with which the modern rifle speaks, and it struck a dull, even a drowsy note upon the air of that languid afternoon of late spring.

"What can that be?" cried Linda.

As if in answer came the sullen far-off sound three times repeated, and then, after an interval, a fourth.

"Shooting!" cried Linda again, very white, her blue eyes wide with terror. "And it's from the direction of Senlis Lake!"

I knew it was and I said what I tried to think.

"It's probably Joe shooting at a bear."

"Joe would not need to fire five times," she answered cogently. "No. Where's Puttick?"

"Ben! Ben Puttick!" roared Petersham.

But loud as was his voice, Linda's call rose higher.

"Here I am!" We heard Puttick's voice from inside the house, and he ran out a minute later.

"We heard five shots from Senlis Lake," I said. "We must start at once, you and I. Mr. Petersham will stay with Miss Linda."

Puttick looked me in the eyes.

"Are you tired of your life?" he asked grimly.

"We have no time to think of that. Get ready!"

"There was five shots," Puttick said deliberately. "I heard 'em myself. That means Joe's dead, if it was him they shot at. If we go we'll soon be dead, too."

"We can't leave him. Come along! We must go to his help."

"Think a bit afore you hurry. If we're shot, they'll come on here." He looked at me.

"Oh, you coward!" cried Linda.

Puttick turned a dull red. "I'm no coward, Miss Linda, but I'm no fool. I'm a woodsman. I know."

"There is a good deal of sense in what Ben says," I put in. "I think his best place is here with you; he shall stay to help you in case of need. I'll go and find Joe. After all, it's as likely as not that he was firing, or perhaps some one else was firing, at a bear."

With the words, I jumped down the verandah steps and ran out along the trail from the clearing. I heard Petersham shouting something, but did not stay to listen; every minute mattered if Joe had really been attacked.

I ran for the first few hundred yards, but then realized that I could not keep up the pace. I knew the general direction of Senlis Lake and made towards it. Fortunately there was a fairly clear trail, upon which I saw here and there the print of moccasins which I took to be Joe's, and later it proved that in this I was right.

I shall not easily forget my race against time, for, to tell the truth, I was sick with fear and the anticipation of evil. Around me spread the beautiful spring woods; here and there grouse sprang whirring away among the pines, the boles of which rose straight into the upper air, making great aisles far more splendid than in any man-built cathedral.

All these things I saw as in a dream, while I hastened forward at the best pace I could attain, until from a rising knoll I caught a glimpse of Senlis Lake. The forest path here rose and fell in a series of short steep inclines. I laboured up these little hills and ran down the slopes. Suddenly I came to a turn and was about to rush down a sharp dip when a voice, seemingly at my side, said:—

"That you, Mr. Quaritch?"

"Joe! Where are you?"

"Here!"

I followed the voice and, parting some branches, saw Joe lying on the ground. His face was grey under its tan, and a smear of blood had dried upon his forehead and cheek.

"You're wounded!" I cried.

"His second passed through the top of my shoulder."

"His? Whose?"

"Him that shot at me."

"Did you shoot back?"

"Sure; he's above there."

"Where?"

"He lies about ten paces west o' that small maple."

"You saw him?"

"Hardly. He had a black hat; I saw it move after he fired his fourth and I shot back. If you'll give me your arm, Mr. Quaritch, we'll go up and take a look at him."

With difficulty and with many pauses, we reached the top of the little ridge. The dead man lay as Joe had said quite near the small maple. The bullet had entered his throat. He was a long-haired, black-bearded man of medium size.

Joe leaned against the maple tree and looked down at him.

"I seem to know the fellow's face," I said.

"Yes, you seen him the day we come, cutting wood by the shack."

"Now, Joe, lean on me, and we'll try to make for home"; for I saw he was very weak.

"Must just look around, Mr. Quaritch. See here! he was smoking his pipe. Look at the ashes—a regular handful of them. He must 'a' lain for me all of a hour before I come along. Here's his rifle; a 30-30. Wonder who he is." Joe lay back panting.

"You're not able to walk," said I. " I'll go back to Kalmacks and get a rig to bring you home."

"No, Mr. Quaritch, it would never be right to do that. It would give the other fellas warning."

"The others?"

"This dead fella's partners."

"You know he has some, then?"

"One, anyway. But let's be moving. Cut me a pole so as I can use it as a crutch."

I did as he asked and we commenced our long and, for him, painful walk back.

As we walked, Joe gave me in little jerks the story of his adventures.

"I started out, Mr. Quaritch," he began.

"Why did you start out? That's what I want to know first of all."

"Seemed like if we didn't get ahead to find out about them fellas soon, something bad might happen."

"You mean you think they would have shot at Miss Petersham?"

"Likely. You see, they was hustling a bit to make Mr. Petersham pay up. Them that fixes blackmail don't like delay; it's apt to be dangerous. I travelled along keeping as good a lookout as might be, but seeing no one. When I got to the Lake I went across to the camp where Bill Worke was fired at—you mind Miss Linda dropped a brooch there?—I had a search for it, but I didn't find it though I come across what I'd hoped to find—a lot of tracks—men's tracks."

"Who had been there since Saturday?"

"Huh! Yes, only about two days old. After a while I built a bit of a fire and cooked a pinch of tea in a tin I'd fetched along. Then after lunk" (Joe always called lunch "lunk"), "I started back. I was coming along easy, not on the path, but in the wood about twenty yards to the south of it, and afore I'd gone above three or four acres, a shot was fired at me from above. The bullet didn't strike me, but as I was in a wonderful poor place for cover,—just three or four spruces and half a dozen sticks of wild raspberry,—I went down, pretending I'd got the bullet, pitched over the way a man does that's got it high up, and I took care to get the biggest spruce trunk between me and where I think the shots come from.

"Sometimes, if you go down like that, a man'll get rattled-like and come out, but not this one. Guess I'm not the first he's put a bit of lead into. He lay still and fired again—got me in the shoulder that time, and I gave a kick and shoved in among the raspberry canes in good earnest; had some of them whitey buds in my mouth and was chewing of them, when the fella shoots twice more—both misses. Then he kind o' paused, and I guesses he's going to move to where he can make me out more clear and let me have it again.

"I see the black hat on him for a moment and then I lets drive. I tried to get up to have a look at him."

"Surely that was risky. How could you know he was dead?"

"Heard the bullet strike and saw the hat go backwards; a man don't never fall over backwards when he's shamming. I couldn't get to him—fainted, I guess. Then you come along."

15
THE CAPTURE

Evening had fallen before we ultimately arrived at Kalmacks. We approached the house with care and entered by a window at the back, as Joe thought it possible the front entrances might be commanded from the wood on that side.

We went at once to the room where Worke was lying and Joe gave him a rapid description of the man he had shot.

"That's Tomlinson," said Worke at once. "Them two brothers lives together. What have they been doing?"

"You'll know afore night," replied Joe. "What are their names?"

"Dandy is the one with the black beard, while him they calls Muppy is a foxy-coloured man."

"Thank you," said Joe. "Now, Bill, if you keep them names to yourself, I'll come back in half an hour and tell you who it was shot you."

On leaving Worke, round-eyed at these words, we went to the living-room, where Petersham and Linda were finishing their supper. On Joe's appearance Linda started up and ran to him.

"You're wounded!" she cried.

"It's nothin' much, Miss Linda."

But as we laid him down on the couch, he seemed to lose consciousness. Petersham brought brandy, and Linda, holding Joe's head upon her arm, put it to his lips. He swallowed some of it and then insisted upon sitting up.

"I must bind up your shoulder—we must stop the bleeding." Linda's distress and anxiety were very evident.

"It's very kind of you, Miss Linda, but here's Mr. Quaritch—he's a bit of a doctor and he'll save you the trouble. It is only a scratch. And there's something we ought to do first."

"The thing we are going to do right now and first is to dress your wound."

And Joe had to give way. With her capable and gentle hands Linda soon dressed the wound and afterwards insisted on sending for Puttick to help him to his bunk. To this, Joe raised no objection.

He was sitting, white of face, propped with cushions when the game-warden entered the room. Puttick gave him a sharp glance.

"So you've got it," said he. "I warned you. Lucky you're not dead."

"Yes, ain't it?" returned Joe.

Well I knew that soft drawl, which November's voice never took except in moments of fiercest tension.

"You'd best join your hands above your head, Ben Puttick. Lock the thumbs. That's right!"

Joe had picked my revolver from the table and held it pointed at Puttick's breast.

"He's mad," screamed Puttick.

"Tie his hands, Mr. Quaritch. Miss Linda, will you please to go away?"

"No, Joe! Do you think I'm frightened?"

"Huh! I know you're brave; but a man acts freer without the women looking on."

Without a word she turned and walked out of the room.

"Puttick's going to confess, Mr. Petersham," went on November.

"I've nothing to confess, you fool!"

"Not even that story you invented about the man with the red hanker across his face . . . the man who wasn't never there ?"

"What's he ravin' about?" cried Puttick.

"Have you forgot them long-haired Tomlinson brothers that . . ."

The effect of this speech on Puttick was instantaneous. Evidently he leaped to the conclusion that he had been betrayed, for

he turned and dashed for the door. We flung ourselves upon him
and by sheer weight bore him to the ground, where we quickly over-
powered him, snarling and writhing.

Some hours later we sat round November Joe who was stretched
upon the couch. Puttick had been tied up and imprisoned in the
strongest room.

"No, Mr. Petersham," Joe was saying. "I don't think you'll have
much more trouble. There was only three men in it. One's dead;
one's locked up, and I dare say we'll find a way of dealing with
number three."

"What I don't understand," said Linda, "is how you found out
that Puttick was in it. When did you begin to suspect him?"

"Last night; when Mr. Petersham didn't go to Butler's Cairn.
The fellas who promised to meet him never put in there either.
That was queer, wasn't it? Of course it could mean just one thing—
that some one had told 'em that Mr. Petersham weren't coming.
There was only us three and Puttick knew. So Puttick must 'a' been
the one to tell."

"But, November," I said, "Puttick never left the house, for you
remember you found no tracks on the sand. How, then, could he
let them know?"

"I guess he waved a lantern or made some other sign they'd
agreed on."

"But why didn't you tell me all this at once?" exclaimed Petersham.

"Because I weren't sure. Their not going to Butler's Cairn *might*
'a' been chance. But this morning, when Puttick comes in with his
yarn about the man with the red hanker across his face, that made
him hold up his hands, and threatened him when he was mending
the canoe, I begun to think we shouldn't be so much longer in the
dark. And when I went down and had a look around by the river, I
knew at once his story was a lie, and that he'd got an interest in
scaring Mr. Petersham away."

"How did you know that?"

"You mind Puttick said the fella come just when he was
beginnin' to mend the canoe? I took a look at the work he'd done

on it and he couldn't 'a' got through all that under an hour. He's fixed a little square of tin over the rent as neat as neat. And then wasn't it queer the fella should have come on him there?—a place he wouldn't be in not one morning of a hundred."

"You believe he made up the whole story? And that no one came at all?"

"I'm pretty sure of it. There wasn't a sign or a track and as to the fella's jumpin' from stone to stone, there's distances of fourteen and sixteen feet between. Still he might 'a' done it, or he might 'a' walked in the water, and I were not going to speak till I were sure."

"Go on. We're still in the dark, Joe," said Linda.

"Well, Miss Linda, you remember how Puttick advised Mr. Petersham to pay or go, and how I told him to stick it out, and when I'd given him that advice, I said to you that I was going across to Senlis Lake, and asked Mr. Quaritch to tell Puttick. I thought there was a good chance that Puttick would put on one of his partners to scare me. You see nobody knew which way I were going but you and him, so it'd be fair certain that if I was interfered with, it would prove Puttick guilty."

"That was clever, though you ran a horrible risk. Was there any particular reason why you chose to go to Senlis Lake?"

"Sure. I wanted to see if any one had been over there looking for your brooch. On'y us and Puttick knew it was lost, and you'd said how your father had paid dollars and dollars for it. When a thing like that's lost, woodsmen'll go miles to try to find it, and Puttick must 'a' told the Tomlinsons, for there was tracks all around our fire where we boiled the kettle."

"Do you think they found my brooch?"

"Huh, no! I pick' it up myself five minutes after you drop' it. I only kep' it, pretendin' it was lost, as a bait like. I've told you what happened to me coming back and how I had to shoot Dandy Tomlinson. His shooting at me after I was down give me a surprise, for I didn't think he'd want to do more than scare me, but I guess it was natural enough, for Puttick was gettin' rattled at me always nosin' round."

"It's all very clear, November, and we know everything except who it was shot Bill Worke."

"I guess Muppy Tomlinson's the man."

"What makes you think that?"

"Bill were shot with a 45-75 Winchester. Both Puttick and Dandy Tomlinson carries 30-30's. Muppy's rifle is a 45-75."

"How can you know what sort of rifle was used to shoot with? The bullet was never found," said Linda.

"I picked up the shell the first time I was over with you."

"And you never told me!" said she. "But that doesn't matter. What I'm really angry with you for is your making me promise not to go out yesterday and then deliberately going out yourself to draw their fire. Why did you do it? If you had been killed I should never have got over it."

"And what 'ud I have done if you'd been killed, Miss Linda?"

"What do you mean, Joe?" said Linda softly.

"I mean that if one of the party I were with got killed in the woods while I was their guide, I'd go right into Quebec and run a boardinghouse or become a politician. That's all I'd be good for!"

16
The City or the Woods?

Although Dandy Tomlinson's bullet had passed through Joe's shoulder, it had left a very ugly wound, but the young woodsman's clean and healthy life stood him in good stead and the process of healing went on rapidly. The chief trouble was his weakness, for he had lost a large amount of blood before I found him.

We had fetched a doctor from Priamville, who left a string of instructions which Linda carried out as closely as she could. Indeed, she would have devoted most of her time to Joe, but he managed to make her spend a good part of each day out of doors. Sometimes he would beg for a fish for his supper and she must catch it herself to prove how well she had profited by his teaching; there were half a hundred things he suggested, not one of which was obvious or trifling, until I marvelled at his ingenuity.

During those days he perforce kept his bunk, where he lay very silent and quiet. I usually found him with his eyes shut as if sleeping, but at the sound of my footstep, if I were alone, he would raise his lashes and look gravely at me.

"You are finding the time long, Joe?" I said on one occasion.

"No, Mr. Quaritch, the hours slip past quick enough. I've never had a lie-by and a while for thinking since I been a man. There's a good few puzzles to life that wants facing one time or another, I s'pose."

"Which puzzle is it that you are facing now?"

"Mr. Petersham wants to be the making of me."

"Then you're about the luckiest young man in this hemisphere!"

"But I have everything I want!. . . Besides, I ain't done nothing for him."

"What about saving his daughter's life?"

"Huh! You'd 'a' done the same."

"I have no particular anxiety to be shot."

Joe shook his head. "If you notioned Miss Linda was to be hurt, you'd not stand off running a bit of a risk to stop it?"

"Perhaps not."

"Just so, and I feel his kindness is more'n I deserve. He'd make me head warden here for a bit first, and then send some kind of a professor to teach me how to talk and fix me up generally." He paused.

"Well, that sounds very reasonable," I commented.

"And after they'd scraped some of the moss off me, he'd put me into his office."

I hid the astonishment I felt at this announcement. "After that?" I asked.

"After that it'd be up to me to make good. He'd help all he knew."

"It sounds a very brilliant future for you, November."

Joe was silent for a moment. "It does, Mr. Quaritch," he said at length in a different tone. "And it gives me something to think about. . . . So they caught Muppy all right? Him and Puttick'll find prison a poor place after the woods."

"I can feel for them," said I, "for I am leaving the woods to-morrow myself. I must get back to Quebec."

He turned his eyes upon me with a look I had never seen in them before.

"That so, Mr. Quaritch?"

"Yes. It is lucky the two men from St. Amiel's have arrived, as it leaves me free to go. The new wardens are sure to be satisfactory, as you recommended them to Mr. Petersham. Besides, all the trouble seems to be over, the squatters are contented enough; the blackmailing plot evidently lay entirely between Puttick and those two scoundrels the Tomlinsons."

"Huh, yes! It was put up among them three, I guess. Kalmacks is safe enough now; there's no call for you to stay longer. Charley Paul and Tom Miller is two good men; I known 'em since I was a boy down to St. Amiel. Mr. Petersham won't never have no better."

"As to that, you'll be here for quite a while yourself."

He made no reply, and when I turned from the window to look at him, he was lying with his eyes closed; and thinking he was tired, I left him.

At the end of the south verandah was situated a small detached room, which we had turned into a workshop, and early the same afternoon I went round there to repair a favourite fishing-rod. The verandah was empty as I passed through it, but presently Petersham joined me.

He did not speak, but sat down in an armchair beside the bench where I was working, and pulling a bundle of letters from his pocket began to open and look them through.

"That fellow, November Joe, is an infernal fool," he said presently. "He is a dolt without an ounce of ambition."

"In his own sphere . . ." I began.

"He is all very well in his own sphere, but he should try to rise above it."

"You think so?"

"Are you mad, James?"

"He has done uncommonly well for himself so far," I said. "He has made good use of his brains and his experience. In his own way he is very, very capable."

"That is true enough, but he has got about as far as he can go without help. As you say, he has done all this for himself. Now I am ready to do a good deal more for him. I'll back him in any line of business he chooses to follow. I owe him that and more. Heaven knows what might have happened to Linda but for him. Those ruffians Puttick and the Tomlinsons were wild to lay hands on money. If Joe had not been here, they would probably have been successful. . . . Perhaps they might have kidnapped her or hurt her in the hope of putting the screw on me!"

"You owe a good deal to November."

"I am well aware of it," replied Petersham. "I am convinced I owe him Linda's life."

Something in his tone showed me his further meaning. I dropped my fishing-rod and stared at him. I knew Linda had enormous influence over her father, but this was beyond imagination.

"You'd never allow it!" I exclaimed.

"Why not?" he retorted angrily. "Isn't Joe better than the Hipper dude? Or Phil Bitshiem . . . or than that—Italian Count with his pedigree from Noah in his pocket? Tell me, where is she going to find a man like Joe? Why, he's got it in him to do things, *big* things, and I hope I'm a good enough Republican not to see the injustice of nailing a fellow down to the spot where he was born."

"But November would never dare look so high! He's modest."

"He'll get over that!"

"I doubt it," I said. "Besides, you are reckoning without Linda . . . how do you know that she . . ."

"Naturally I don't know for sure about Linda," he answered shortly; then glancing at his watch he got up. "Just about time to get my mail ready."

We had been speaking in low tones, for the subject of our conversation naturally did not lend itself to loud talk, and besides, during the last quarter of an hour or so a murmur of voices from the verandah had warned us to be careful. We had not shut the door leading to the verandah, as it was the only one, and we needed it open for light and air. Petersham walked towards it, but, instead of stepping out, he turned and laid a hand like a vice on my arm.

"Quiet! Quiet for your life!" he whispered. "She must never know we were here!"

"But, Joe, you're mistaken, Joe . . . I wish it!" It was Linda's voice, shy and trembling as I had never heard it.

"Ah, that's all your great goodness, Miss Linda, and I haven't earned none of it."

I pointed frantically to the door . . . we must shut that door and shut out those voices, but Petersham swore at me under his breath.

"Darn! you know those hinges screech like a wildcat! It can't be helped, for it would kill her to know we heard a word of this."

We crept away into the farthest corner of the workshop, but even there phrases floated to us, though mercifully we could not hear all. "But father would help you, for you know you are a genius, Joe."

"All I could ever do lies in the woods, Miss Linda; woodsways is the whole of it. A yard outside the wood, and the meanest chap bred on the streets could beat me easy. I can't thank you nor Mr. Petersham the way I'd like to, for my tongue is slow . . ." Here his voice fell.

A period of relief came to me; for some minutes the interchange of speech, low and earnest as it was, reached us only in a vague murmuring.

"But if you hate the city life so much, you must not go to the city," —it was Linda again. "Live your life in the woods . . . I love the woods too."

"The woods is bleak and black enough to them that's not born among the trees. Them that's lived outside allus wants more, Miss Linda. The change of colour, the fall o' the leaf, the snow, by 'n by the hot summer under the thick trees—that's all we wild men want. But it's different for them that's seen all the changes o' the big world beyond."

A long interval followed before the voices became audible again. "Oh, no, no, Joe!"

Petersham clutched my arm once more at the sound.

"You're so young, Miss Linda, you don't know. . . . I'd give my right hand to believe different, but I can't! It wouldn't be best . . . not for you."

November's tone moved me more than Linda's passion. He was a man fighting it out against his own heart. I knew well the power of attraction Linda possessed, but somehow I had not guessed how it had worked on Joe. When I came to think of it, I understood how blind I had been, that the influence was inevitable. It was not only her beauty, it was more than that. November, untaught woodsman though he might be, had found in her the answering note to his own high nature. I had, indeed, been right in so far that he had not dreamed of aspiring to her; nevertheless the episode would mean pain and loss to him, I feared, for many a day.

Once more I heard him.

"Don't you think I'll be proud every hour I have to live that you was so good to me, Miss Linda? I shan't never forget it."

"Joe, I think I hate you!" she cried, and then the quick tap of her footsteps told us she had run into the house.

There was absolute silence for a minute or two. At length Joe sighed heavily, and with the slow laborious movement of weakness went to his room.

When all seemed safe, Petersham and I stole out of hiding like thieves, and, though we exchanged no word, Petersham was swearing violently under his breath until he shut his office door.

Rather to my surprise, November Joe came out for a while after supper, because he said it was my last evening at Kalmacks. Neither he nor Linda gave any sign that anything unusual had passed between them. Indeed, we were gay enough and we had Charley Paul in to sing us some French-Canadian songs.

After saying good-bye as well as good-night to Linda and her father, I followed Joe to his room.

"I won't wake you up in the morning, November," I said. "There's nothing like rest and sleep to put you on your legs again."

"I've been trying that cure, Mr. Quaritch, and I won't be long behind you."

"Oh, where are you going to?"

"To my shack on Charley's Brook. I'm kind o' homesick-like, and that's the truth."

"But how about Mr. Petersham's wish to give you a start in his business in New York or Montreal?"

"I'm not the kind of a guy for a city, Mr. Quaritch. All the chaps'd get turning round to stare at the poor wild fella, and I'd sure be scairt to sleep in one of them up-in-the-blue-sky houses, anyway!" He laughed.

"But you would soon be used to city ways, and perhaps become a great man and rich!"

"That was what the mink said to the otter. 'Go you to the city and see the sights,' says he, but the otter knew the only way he'd ever see the city would be around some lovely gal's neck."

November Joe had no idea how far I could read into his fable.

"And what did the otter say?"

"Huh! Nothing. He just went down his slide into the lake and got chasin' fish, and I guess he soon forgot he missed seein' the city, all right."

"And how about you, Joe?"

"I guess I'll get chasin' fish, too, Mr. Quaritch."

When I arrived at the depot at Priamsville in the morning, to my surprise I found November Joe there before me.

"Why, Joe!" I exclaimed, "you're not fit to travel."

"I thought I'd go on the cars with you, Mr. Quaritch, if you'll have me. There's a good many times to change before we gets to Silent Water, and I'm not so wonderful quick on my feet yet."

"You'd better come right through to Quebec," I said, "and let my sister feed you up for a few days."

But he insisted on leaving me at Silent Water, and I sent a wire to Mrs. Harding to look after him. During the journey, I spoke several times of Kalmacks, but November had little or nothing to say in reply.

He soon grew strong again and he wrote me of his trapping and shooting, so at any rate he is trying to forget all that he renounced at Kalmacks. But will Linda have no further word to say? And if she . . .

I wonder.

Coachwhip Publications

CoachwhipBooks.com

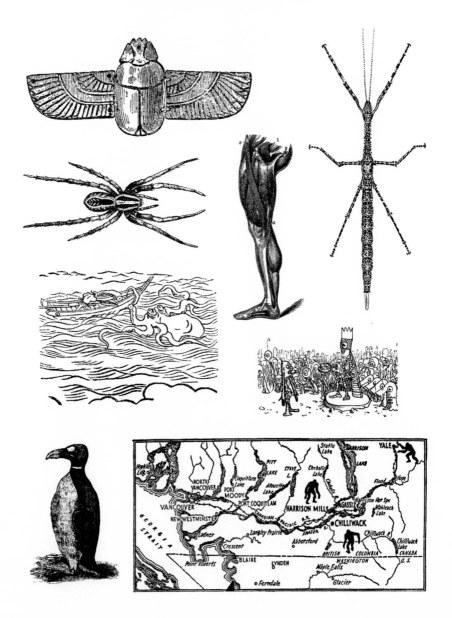

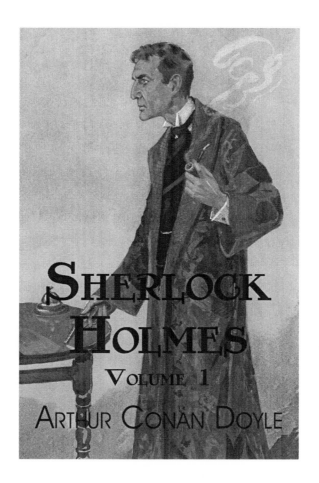

SHERLOCK HOLMES

Volume 1: ISBN 1-61646-006-7

Volume 2: ISBN 1-61646-007-5

Volume 3: ISBN 1-61646-008-3

Mystery and Detection with

THE THINKING MACHINE

Volume I

JACQUES FUTRELLE

THE THINKING MACHINE

Volume 1: ISBN 1-930585-70-5

Volume 2: ISBN 1-930585-71-3

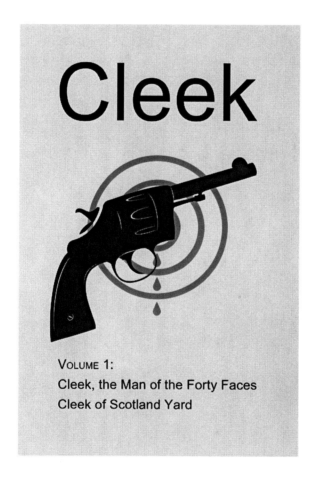

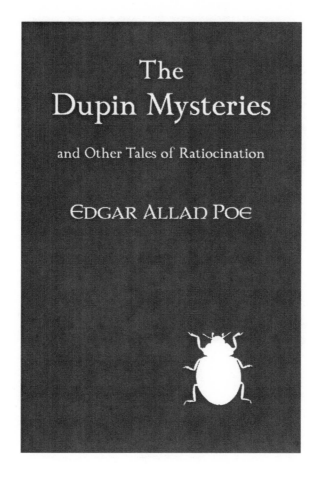

The
Dupin Mysteries

and Other Tales of Ratiocination

EDGAR ALLAN POE

EDGAR ALLAN POE'S
THE DUPIN MYSTERIES

ISBN 1-930585-69-1

AN AFRICAN MILLIONAIRE

ISBN 1-61646-014-8

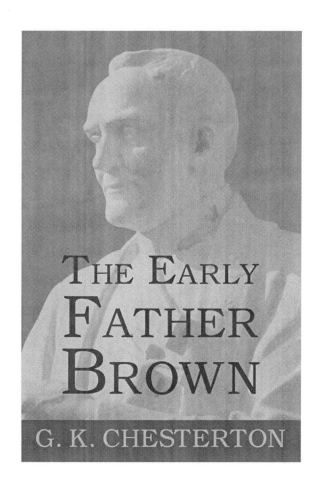

THE EARLY FATHER BROWN

ISBN 1-61646-012-1